THE

GRAVE

An intense, gripping crime thriller

DIANE M DICKSON

THE
BOOK
FOLKS

Paperback published by The Book Folks

London, 2019

ISBN 978-1-0938-5662-0

www.thebookfolks.com

For my family.

Chapter 1

Samuel struggled through the roots and brambles; he tripped often and grovelled in the dark tearing his trousers on the thorns. In time he reached the place, down on the bank, where the ground was damp and smelled of moss and decay. At the base of a massive willow he threw his load to the ground and paused to catch his breath.

When he knew for sure that he hadn't been followed, he bent to the task. The moon shone silver through dark branches as he turned the sod. With each swing of the long-handled pick, a grunt escaped his gut; deep and sonorous in the quiet. Muscles in his back and shoulders flexed and strained and he stopped often to wipe the dirty sweat that ran across his brow and stung his eyes. He stood back occasionally to assess the work, shaking his head at the small results of his efforts.

Though time was short he had to have it deep enough to deny access to the wild things. The arc of the pick glinted as it caught the moonlight over and over, and the ground opened a great maw that took him in further than his knees, further than his hips. He was getting there. Now he used the spade, the better to scoop the dank soil and toss it onto the growing heap.

A shrill note tore into the silence, sharp and shocking. He thrust again with the blade and again the noise rang out assaulting the silence as metal struck stone. He peered into the murk to see a boulder gleaming white, like a tooth in a blackened and receding gum-line.

With a grunt of impatience, he knelt in the soggy pit and groped at the boulder digging and pulling till his nails tore and his fingers bled. The mud and the blood congealed, clubbing the ends of his fingers and he wiped them on the tail of his shirt, cursing as the sticky gobbets smeared the fabric.

At last it was deep enough and he dragged the bundled tarpaulin to the lip of the grave. Kneeling in the mud he half pushed, half lowered the thing, shifting and dragging at the bulk, fighting with the cascading earth and the crumbling edges. Finally, dizzy with exhaustion he threw the last measure of earth back onto the grave thumping and flattening it with the back of his shovel.

It still wasn't enough, now he went upstream a little to find small shrubs. Bringing them back with great clods of earth still sticking to the shocked roots, he planted them onto the mound. It was not some bizarre parody of funeral ritual but a ploy to further disguise the newly dug earth and to consolidate the disturbed ground.

Hours had passed and the dawn was threatening but the job was finished. He dragged his bent and aching body through the mists and the damp and left his terrible secret in the unmarked hollow amongst the willows, beside the river.

Chapter 2

He turned to home. Before he arrived at the shack the sun had risen and the first day of his altered world had begun. The next task was to take the tools to the small lean-to and wash the blades. He polished and dried the metal and hung the equipment back in its proper place, all in order, all as it should be. No sign of the turmoil and terror of the dark hours.

The house was cold, the fire had long deadened and he had left the door open, allowing the damp and dew of early morning to enter.

A galvanised bucket stood beneath the sink and Samuel ran water into it, adding bleach from a big plastic bottle. He reached back into the dark space feeling around for the scrubbing brush. The tender parts at the end of his fingers caught on the rough wood causing him to let out a hiss of pain and a curse that echoed through the quiet of the old rooms.

The stain was extensive, it had missed the rug but had spread and run along the grain of scuffed floor boards, pooling at the skirting. First, he dipped a large rag into the water and slopped it into the congealing gore. The glutinous mixture splashed back at him, he felt the wet sliminess on his face and dashed at it with the back of his hand. The smell of the bleach was strong in his nose but it was a clean scent after the muck by the river and the freshness surrounded him as he now knelt on the bloodstained floor. He sloshed more water from the cloth but it simply spread the contamination and it was obvious to him now he would need to sluice the entire surface.

He dragged the chairs and table to the rear of the room and rolled up the rugs, throwing them through the open doorway out onto the porch. Too late he realised he would need to brush the liquid out that way. Anger drove him on and for a moment he was overwhelmed by the whole thing. It was unbelievable to him that he had allowed this to happen; he had worked hard to escape such stuff and yet here he was again wallowing in the detritus of death.

After a long moment he took a sharp breath and squared his shoulders. Reaching for the cheap floor covering, he grabbed at the fraying edges and heaved the bundle as hard and as far as he could; it thudded into the bushes by the well. He turned his back on it, *let it rot*.

He picked up the pail of cooling water and flung it across the floor. The mix spread, painting the boards pink now with small clots caught on the rougher edges. It had been left too long, had taken a hold, wanting to become a part of the fabric of this cursed place.

The stiff brush was in the lean-to and, as he made his way through the yard, clouds of condensation swirled around his head, and the cold, sharp morning mocked him with normality.

After several minutes of effort, scrubbing, sluicing and brushing, the floor was darkened with moisture, but cleared of the obvious signs of brutality. Taking a bottle from the dresser, he dragged out the cork and stomped to the front steps where he dropped onto his behind on the damp wood. The rough whisky burned in his throat and seared a river of heat all the way down into his gut where it swilled with the bile and threatened reflux and nausea. He swallowed another mouthful and it settled his stomach and flamed in his blood, deadening the sharp edges of his nerves and stroking and soothing his rattling senses. He had to think now, he had to be logical and calm; be sure, absolutely sure there was no trace, no trail and if need be, he would have to be ready to act again.

He could see no way the body would be found, not where it lay beside the river, deep in the wood; only a very pernicious fate would reveal it. But he knew only too well just how malign chance could be and he acknowledged the risk; accepted it was probably only a question of when, not if.

Chapter 3

Physical exertion, stress and despair blended now with the alcohol wrapping around his brain, clouding his thinking and stupefying him. Samuel reached out and, grabbing the door frame for support, he dragged himself to his feet. With a yell, part animal, part human but full of anguish he drew back his arm, the empty whisky bottle flipped end over end through the morning air to land with a thud and a sharp crack. By the time the sound reached his ears he had already turned to stagger back into the dank living room.

The furniture was piled haphazardly against the back wall of the space, he ignored it except where he leaned to aid his unsteady progress. The banister creaked with the weight as he dragged himself up the bare stairs towards the tumbled and untidy bed. He threw himself across the tangled sheets and turned onto his side. Drawing a pillow across, he buried his face and was lost in the smell of her, the sweetness of manufactured perfume and the natural stench of animal fluids mixed as they could only be after the passion of just a few hours ago.

He was swept with anger and bitterness and beneath it all disappointment that even one small loosening of the grip he had on his life had betrayed him so catastrophically. He knew though that to rail against fate was pointless. With a deep sigh he closed his eyes and let exhaustion and alcohol carry him away. He drifted into uneasy slumber, tossing and mumbling on the bed as the world wound down the day.

* * *

Scarlet streaks banded the darkening sky before he woke. Pushing up from the bed and making his way stiff-legged and robotic to the bathroom, he relieved himself. He turned to the wash basin and caught a glimpse of his face in the mirror.

There was blood and mud streaked across his cheeks and chin. There were scratches there too, great wheals torn by the thorns of the forest. The skin had become puckered and was reddened already with a small infection. He tore off his shirt, ran water into the bowl and washed his face and head, letting the cool liquid run down his back and chest to wet the waistband of his filthy trousers. It was no use though; he needed to strip, shower and clean himself. With a sigh he dragged the clothes away from his aching body, flinging them into a stinking pile in the corner of the room. He turned the water to hot and waited until steam billowed from the tub before stepping under the deluge.

It helped; sore muscles softened and relaxed, and his brain cleared a little. The gushing water isolated him from the sights and sounds in the house and allowed his mind to go back for the first time to yesterday morning. Bright sunshine had encouraged the trip to town, the weekly run for provisions and a glass of beer in the company of other people. He knew he would have to look at it, revisit the event and then put it away for the rest of his existence; so why not start now, in the comfort of warm water and behind the screen of steam and the plastic curtain?

He should have ignored the woman, he had always done so before, why then did this one who was barely more than a girl manage to draw him in?

"Buy me a drink, mister. Do you want some company? I'll sit with you, talk, not talk – up to you."

Normally he would turn away, they would get the message and move on but this time, he simply threw some coins across the counter and jerked a thumb towards her for the benefit of the barman.

She slipped onto the high stool, sipped the glass of white wine and then slid around to gaze with round, blue eyes at him. First the big hands, work-worn, permanently ingrained with dirt, finger nails torn and cracked. Then up to his sullen, lined face.

"You're Samuel, aren't you?"

He nodded, a sharp jerky movement, already regretting the drink and the unspoken invitation.

"You live in the woods, yeah, out there on your own. I've seen you around, you seem lonely, are you lonely Samuel, do you need company?"

Her thin hand had moved to his thigh, rubbing a little against the denim. He reached down and, not roughly but purposively, he moved it and placed it back in the girl's lap. He slid from the stool and without another word walked out of the bar. That had been a mistake, it had spoiled the trip and now he needed to get back home.

He walked to the builder's yard to collect a roll of wire to repair the fence, then he crossed the street and strode back to the car park. She was standing beside the truck, one foot up against a tyre, her knee bent, bony in the tight pants. She was smoking and as he approached, she threw the unfinished cigarette to the ground scuffing it with the sole of her knee-high boots. "Will you give me a ride, Samuel? I need a ride."

Chapter 4

He stood beside the car, and looking down at her, shook his head.

"I'm late, I need to get back, go and ask one of the others, there's plenty in there'll give you a ride."

He jerked his thumb towards the bar.

"Oh, now that's not gentlemanly, is it? I won't take you far out of your way, come on now, don't you want to help a damsel in distress? It's getting late now."

It was true he had stayed longer than normal, eaten lunch waiting for some maintenance on the chainsaw, normally he would have been long gone by now, safe back in the woods.

"You don't want to ride with me, now go on back there."

He strode past and leaned to unlock the door. She placed a hand over his.

"Samuel, I like you, I've seen you around town before, you always seem so lonely. Don't you want some company? Come on just give me a little ride, you can drop me at the bus station, if you like."

He pushed her sharply out of the way, a heel caught on the rough surface of the car park and she toppled, snatching out at him as she fell. He grabbed at the flailing hand but at the end she was kneeling in the dirt, her hand grazed and jeans soiled with mud. He was caught now, couldn't just walk away, he hadn't meant her to fall but he couldn't just leave her.

He helped her up, she wasn't hurt apart from the few small scratches; she sucked at the beading of blood, looking up under her lashes, and she knew she had him now.

He moved the parcels from the passenger seat and unhooked the seat belt from the stowage point. His heart was pounding, he hadn't wanted this, didn't want this, but he would cope. He could deal with it, to the edge of town, the bus stop, and then it would be over and next week he would ignore her if she was there; if she spoke to him. He started the engine and turned towards the road, his hands shook on the steering wheel.

The sniffling started after a couple of minutes, at first he thought it was shock brought on by the tumble, but it had been such a small thing. He turned to look at her face in the flashing orange of the street lamps; mascara had drawn black runnels down her cheeks. She was trying to squeeze her bleeding hand into the tightness of the jeans pocket. He handed her a clean rag that he kept on the dashboard for wiping the screen. She nodded her thanks and blew her nose loudly.

"I'm sorry, sorry Samuel."

A great sigh filled the uncomfortable silence between them.

"Are you hurt, more than that little thing I mean?"

"No, no I'm alright."

"Why are you crying then?"

"I don't know why you don't like me, why don't you like me, Samuel? Nobody ever seems to like me."

His knuckles were tight now on the wheel, his fingers wrapped all the way round, the muscles bunching in his forearms. Sweat had popped out under his hairline. He had to get her out of the car; he pulled over to the kerb.

"Get out, go on, you're not hurt; I don't want you in the car, don't want you here."

He leaned to open the passenger door and she caught at his arm.

"Oh come on now, don't be like that. You know we could have a bit of fun you and me, we could. I could make you relax; I think you need to relax."

She stroked at his skin, irritating the small hairs He snatched his arm back.

He turned, twisting in his seat to look straight at her. The blonde hair swung as she swivelled her face towards him and reached again for his arm.

"Come on now, Samuel, a fine man like you, you should have some fun, let yourself relax. Don't you want to have a bit of fun? That's all it'd be, no strings, no comeback, just a nice night together. What about it?"

That was the point, he saw it now, now it was too late, that was the moment all was lost. She was soft and pretty and it had been years; well of course it had been years.

He had never enjoyed sex with a hooker, never wanted some brutalised whore who was busy thinking about her next score while he pumped away above her, but this girl, she had sparkling eyes, soft lips and it had been so very long. She would want something from him afterwards, money probably and so really little better than a whore but she had searched him out, it made a difference. He could feel his body pleading, his brain and common sense at odds with each other.

He slipped the car into gear and drove off past the pharmacy, past the streetlights, past the point of no return.

Chapter 5

There had been little conversation on the drive to the shack, Samuel was too tense and wound up; he had spoken once.

"So, what's your name, seeing as you know mine already?"

"Sylvie, I'm Sylvie, nice to meet you, Samuel."

She had held a hand towards him, a grin on her face but he didn't look at her and with a shrug she let it drop back into her lap – the silence resumed. For a long time she gazed through the window at the darkening silhouettes of trees and fence posts flicking away behind the car as it grumbled on over the tarmac. The occasional signpost would flash a bright message into the gloom and the houses they passed glowed like little oases with the lawns touched green under lamps and security lights, otherwise all was dark and quiet.

A few cars hissed by, the occupants heading for a night in the town and one van overtook them. She watched the tiny rubies of its tail lights fading into the black until it turned a distant bend and became a memory.

"How far is your place, I know it's in the woods, but how far?"

"Not far now, a few minutes that's all."

They turned in from the road and the darkness was deeper, much deeper than she had thought it would be. The track was rutted and winding and she hung on to the sides of the seat as they bumped and jolted into the woods. The way was a tunnel lit only by the headlights, now and again a creature would leap or scutter from their path, a sharp intrusion, there and gone in a flash. Apart from the roar of the engine, the sounds now were all those of nature and of night in the woods.

He swung left and the road ran beside the river for a brief spell. The dark water glinted as the moon caught the ripples but the gently flowing ribbon was mysterious and she turned away from the window. She watched him, the shape of his head and shoulders, tense and unfriendly; she wondered nervously what she had done. The idea had seemed good in the town; she'd been filled with bright light bravado but now was unsure. It was further than she had thought it would be; she would have to be sure he left the keys in the car, even then didn't know whether she would be able to find her way back alone.

Maybe she should let the plan go, just have the sex and ask him for payment; he must know money was what it was all about, or at least he should understand that. She would wait, play it as it came, let things develop, but for sure this dark and forbidding place wasn't what she had imagined. Parks and playgrounds had been the only natural spaces she had known, the woods at night were not what she had expected.

Chapter 6

As the car drew into the yard Samuel jumped from the door, leaving Sylvie to clamber down on her own. By the time she joined him he had his provisions piled beside the steps.

"Shall I lock the car for you?"

He looked at her askance.

"Why the hell would I lock the car, who do you think is going to take it out here?"

He turned and climbed the wooden stairs, slipping the keys into the pocket of his jeans. At least she knew where they were and knew the old Land Rover wasn't locked. Her mouth was dry and her palms damp; this had been a bad idea. Hell, it hadn't even been a proper idea. She had seen him, remembered the talk and decided to try and get to him and then see where it led. Some vague notion of lifting valuables and then running had tickled at the back of her mind. She knew he lived in the woods but had never had any idea just how far out of town it was, no-one had ever said. She had assumed a couple of miles, walking distance at a pinch, not this great trek away from the lights and the houses and all she was used to. How could anyone live out here?

The talk in town could be all wrong of course; they had said he had money. That he was a rich recluse, eccentric, but this place gave lie to all of it. It was ramshackle, simple and sparse. She had expected a pretty cottage, perhaps something even grander, but this was little more than a hut, the floors were bare and the kitchen simple and old fashioned.

She had listened to the idle chatter and this is not what it had said. He had come to the town just a few years ago, no-one knew where from, no-one knew anything. He kept himself to himself except on a rare occasion when he would say a few words about the weather or suchlike. That he didn't seem to work but always had money in his pocket and paid for everything in cash led to rumours of riches hidden at his place. Where the money had come from was never made clear but no-one doubted its existence; and so here she was.

In her mind now were several options. Maybe she could get him to give her money, if he liked her enough – if she gave him a good enough time. It wouldn't be much though, she had approached him; he would probably think she was on the game and want to pay her whatever he felt the sex was worth. She could tell him a sob story, God knew her life was full of those, maybe she could appeal to his kindness. From what she'd seen though there wasn't much of that about this man. The other option, the most daring, the one she had in mind back in town, was to take what she could and run.

Now though, she saw it had been stupid, she had assumed there would be a safe, a desk, articles around she could hide in her bag, but this bare and simple place held nothing of value, whatever money he had it hadn't been spent on comfort. Maybe there wasn't any – no money, no treasures, nothing; just a dirty, scary, curmudgeonly man and bare boards. The thought depressed her, she had made mistakes before, so many mistakes and this looked to be just another one, another stupid half-baked idea, doomed to failure even before it began. Tears stung her eyes and she felt ready to cry in earnest now. She turned from him and gulped back the misery. She'd make the best of it now. She'd have to.

Chapter 7

He looked at the girl, she was young, muscles still trim, skin smooth and warm. It had been a long time and now Samuel hoped for no more than physical release. She laughed and stroked at his skin, raked her fingers through his hair. She had poured them both whiskies while he stowed the shopping and then dragged him up to the bedroom. If she found the space unappealing, he couldn't tell. She threw herself across the bed, her legs waving in the air as she pulled off her jeans and threw aside the cheap sweater. Her bra and pants were skimpy and covered little of the small body.

He was taken aback by the girl's enjoyment. Even though she had made the move on him in town, he'd assumed she was simply out for money, not for this, not for pleasure. He tried to shake off his earlier misgivings and found himself smiling as she wiggled across the covers, in her underwear. She patted the mattress and crooked a finger at him. Maybe it would be okay, perhaps she really did like him after all. The smile felt odd on his face, it didn't fit the fall of his muscles and his eyes filled for a moment. It had been so long, so long since he had felt pleasure, so long since he had felt anything other than breathing, dragging from one day to the next.

Living alone he didn't acknowledge loneliness, that would be an emotion and he quelled and quashed anything other than the slight pleasure he took from the birds, the trees and the quiet river. Before, he had let emotion rule him and he knew too well it was a traitor and would do him no good.

Looking down at this young body, the long legs crossed at the ankles and her slender arms flexing as she raised the glass to her lips, he felt himself stirring and the sense of living took his breath away. He dropped his clothes to the floor and lowered himself onto the bed beside her, still wearing his shorts, tightening now as evidence of his growing passion. She ran a finger round the waist band and slid them away from his backside.

They enjoyed each other, at least Samuel believed they did. She giggled and writhed and gave as well as taking, he let her set the pace and, once he had relaxed, it was easy and fun. He was still afraid but not as much now and at the end as he lost himself in the moment he was as he once had been, a man and only that – no pain, no guilt and no sorrow.

They wrapped themselves in towels and went to the kitchen, he cooked eggs and toast, and sitting on the old couch they drank whisky and smiled at each other.

Not lovers, not even friends, but now more than strangers.

"Where do you live, Sylvie, are you from the town?"

She nodded at him, her mouth full of eggs and toasted bread, "Yeah, born there, never been many places, never had the chance. No job, not much to do and I'm not clever or anything. What about you, where are you from?" A cloud swept through his eyes and he stood and carried the plates back into the kitchen, but he made no response.

"Will you want me to take you back? To town, tonight I mean? Will you be missed?"

"Nah, there's nobody to miss me, Mum and Dad have moved away. I live in a flat above the betting office. I can stay, if you like, I don't have to but it's a long drive back, we can leave it till tomorrow."

"Why didn't you go, with your mum and dad?"

"We didn't get on here and I didn't see how being somewhere else would make a difference and they were going to live by my nan. All old people, minding my business, nagging at me. I'm better here."

He simply nodded, he understood the value of being alone. Maybe this girl would be good to know, maybe when he went into town he could meet her sometimes, chat. He had to ask about the other thing though, what she wanted, what was expected from him now. He still couldn't believe she had simply come with him for fun.

"Do you need some money, something, if you've no job?"

He didn't know what he hoped for, the truth would do, at least not offence, and he felt he owed her now. She had made him remember what it felt like to be alive, how could you pay for that? He didn't know.

"Well, I suppose if you're offering."

He was saddened, had hoped for something else, but tried not to let it show.

"How about I take you back in the morning and then I can give you something, you know, for your time?"

She simply nodded and it was settled. She stood and walked to him, the towel fell to the floor and she giggled as he grabbed at it, dragging it back over her nakedness.

"Come on, Samuel, let's go and get warm again."

She led him by the hand back to the bedroom.

Chapter 8

The moon was caught in the trees outside the uncurtained window, the silvery luminescence was enough to show her the dark shapes in the simple room and the hump of the man sleeping now on the other side of the thin mattress. He was breathing deeply, his mouth was open a little. One arm was cast above his head the bulk of it squashing the pillow, the other draped over her chest, just below the level of her breasts; she took in shallow breaths, trying not to disturb him.

In the pale light she could make out his hair, the gleam of skin on his forehead and the darker colour of his lips. He wasn't a bad looking man, older than anyone else she had been with, but she had been surprised by his tenderness and even more by his gratitude. When he had looked down at her and she saw the glisten of tears on his lashes, she had to turn away, feeling her heart change.

She didn't know him, she couldn't say whether or not she liked him, certainly being with him was different, but it had not been the way she had expected. They had talked little; she had tried but had not been able to draw any information from him. Though they had been as close physically as two humans could be, she still did not know where he came from, who his family might be; she still didn't even know him by any other name than Samuel.

Staring through the window at the dark trees and the beautiful moon she was swept with sadness. She had intended simply to take from him, money yes, and whatever else she could get. Now, in the darkness it was possible to realise the idiocy of her plan, there was no way to take his money, if indeed he had any. No way for her to drive the big old Land Rover and find her way back through the terrifying darkness of the woods beside the pewter slide of the river. Again, yet again, she had made stupid decisions, acted without thinking and now here she was lying in this strange, plain room with a man who more and more she was beginning to like but about whom she knew nothing.

She shook her head, what a fool she could be at times. With a gentle finger she stroked a lock of hair back from his forehead. No, she would take from him only the pleasure he had given her tonight and maybe there would be a chance to know him better and perhaps he could be a friend. God knew she needed friends, especially now.

She had told him there was no-one in the town to miss her. She had lied.

Chapter 9

Sylvie drifted back into her dreams, almost sleeping, comfortable with the thoughts she'd just had. Happier now the decision was made to do something good, something kind.

The flash of light across the walls and ceilings almost passed her by, it was an instant of change, but somewhere her safety mechanism registered the difference in illumination and she stirred. Her eyes were wide in the darkness and although at this moment she couldn't really name the cause of alarm, the knowledge that there was something wrong made her heart pound. Samuel slept on; she slithered carefully out from under his casual embrace. Through the woods now came quite clearly the rumble of an engine and even at this early stage she felt deep in her gut that this was trouble coming. She was no stranger to trouble and sliding her feet from under the thin covers she pulled on her shirt and braced herself to face it.

The engine noise stopped and, as expected, it was superseded by the slam of a door and the crunch of shoes on the broken path outside. She flew on bare feet from the dim room and ran down the stairs. Hanging on to the banister for support her nerves jangled and jolted with fear of what she thought she knew. By the time she had reached the door and dragged it open he was there, his hand raised to knock. Thank God she had got there in time, maybe Samuel would sleep through this, maybe she could deal with it, handle the situation and he would never know.

She stepped onto the wooden balcony.

It was Phil, she recognized the skinny body, the hunch of his shoulders and the quick, short stride. He'd bring her grief, he always did.

"Phil, how did you get here, how did you know?"

There was no answer save the slap of his hand across her cheek. It wasn't a hard blow and not a surprise, though the sting of it made her gasp. It had always been a part of him, meanness and casual brutality; it was just who and what he was.

"Bitch, what the hell are you doing?"

Another slap, she couldn't help herself, she cried out.

"Stupid bitch, Benny saw you getting in the weirdo's car, he came to find me, do you think I like that? Do you bitch? Do you think you can make me a laughing-stock, behaving like a bloody whore?"

She knew his standing amongst his mates mattered more than she ever would. She was his woman but a woman could be replaced, his reputation, his street cred could not.

Another blow aimed now at her belly, bringing her to her knees. She knew he had held back, knew from past experience he wouldn't let go yet, wouldn't use all his strength not until he had toyed with her a while, taken his full revenge.

She looked up at him; the tears ran from her eyes, cold on the stinging skin of her reddening cheek.

"Phil, don't. Please don't, I'll explain, I was out to get some money, I thought I could kid him, you know pinch some stuff. I didn't know it was going to be like this. I thought he'd have a posh house and I had no idea how far it was from town. Listen to me Phil, don't make a noise, come on let's go. Let me get my bag, and then we'll go."

He glanced around and then stepped in close, invading her space. She could smell the alcohol on his breath, stale smoke on his clothes and in his hair. It was hard to breathe.

"So, you came to rob him, well where's the stuff, where's the money?"

"There isn't any, least I don't think so, look at this place, look at it. There's no money, there's nothing to take. Come on let's go back, I made a mistake Phil. Just a mistake."

"Yeah, you can say that again." He stepped back and turned from her for an instant and then he twisted and spun. He raised his leg in a vicious karate kick. His trainer connected with the side of her chest. She yelped in pain.

Now, the door swung back on its hinges crashing against the old wood of the walls. There he stood. In the light from the car headlights Samuel looked enormous, the night was filled with the sound of his breathing and the look on his face chilled her to the depth of her being. She had never seen such anger.

He didn't speak. He reached out and grabbed the youth by both shoulders dragging him into the room. Flinging him backwards he watched coldly as the yob crashed into the threadbare couch. Samuel raised his powerful arm and crashed it downwards. If it had found its mark, then surely it would have smashed the skull of the man cowering before him.

Phil rolled to his knees, pushing himself upright. He skittered across the room, nippy like a rat, quicksilver in his fear.

Samuel was after him, striding over the boards, his fists clenched, shoulders bunched, his bulky body full of the fight.

Phil backed off as far as he could and spread his hands behind him across the kitchen worktop; his fingers seeking and clawing for a weapon. He glanced round, there it was. The knife was lying on the chopping board, it wasn't large but it was sharp. The scrawny hand closed over the handle and now, crouched in a position that was second nature to him, Phil turned to the older, bigger man and snarled.

"Come on then, big man, you want some of me, come and get it."

They were deaf to the screams of Sylvie sobbing and begging from the doorway. Locked in a duel as old as time, they had both acknowledged this could only end with one of them down, the other victorious. There would be no handshake, no surrender and no chance of peace now until this thing had reached an end.

Phil jabbed forward with the knife extended, feinting and dodging, his feet spread wide, knees bent. In response Samuel stood before him tensed and watchful.

It was over quickly. He judged his timing and then, without hesitation and seemingly with no pause for reflection, Samuel began to move and then just ploughed on. Like a juggernaut he barrelled into the smaller man. Phil was used to street fighting, circling and hissing, sizing up his opponent, as much about effect as result and he hadn't time to readjust his thinking. Samuel dragged the knife from his hand, brute force, unstoppable in fury. He spun Phil around and dragged him back with his free hand pinning the squirming body against his heaving chest. He sliced once, then back the same way, all his strength behind the hand holding the weapon.

Blood pumped from Phil's neck, soaking his clothes and washing downwards to his shoes. He raised a sticky hand now before his shocked face and then, in just moments, he crumpled gargling from his useless throat. He convulsed, his eyes wild but even now unseeing as he bled out onto the floor. For a breathless while all that could be heard was Sylvie whimpering from the place near the door where she had become a quivering heap.

Chapter 10

Samuel stepped from the shower and rubbed at himself with the thin towel. It was time now to move. There was nothing to be gained from going over it again, what had happened was fact and it was done.

He had pulled the quivering shape of Sylvie from the floor where she was crouched, hiding behind hands wet with tears.

"Who the hell is he, you told me there was no-one?"

"I'm sorry, I'm sorry. Samuel, it's Phil, he's, well, oh I don't know, he's my boyfriend I suppose, but I kept trying to get away from him. He won't let me go, he gets so jealous. Oh God, is he dead?"

As she spoke she backed against the wall, attempting to put as much space as possible between herself, the body and the spreading pool of blood.

"He is, isn't he? God, Samuel he's dead. What are you going to do?"

"Deal with it."

The answer was so sharp, so lacking in emotion that for a moment she simply stared at him, silent.

"How, how can you deal with it? We'll go to jail. They'll lock us up."

He ran a hand through his hair, blood smeared on his forehead. She couldn't bear to see it so she buried her face in her hands again and began sobbing. He reached out to her and drew her forward. Wrapped in his arms she gulped and hiccupped and then after a while the crying stopped. Now she was calmer he bent close and spoke to her, his voice was low and serious but he sounded calm and certain. It helped.

"Get your things, take the car, you can drive, right?"

She nodded.

"Okay, do you think you can find your way back to town?"

Again she gave a small nod.

"Go back to your place, behave as though everything is normal. If anyone asks, tell them you haven't seen him. Do you understand?"

A nod.

"What are you going to do though, Samuel?"

"You don't need to know, I'll deal with it, I've told you. Now just go. Later, tonight, I'll come into town. I need to get away; I'll have to go. You can come if you want. If you don't want to you may have to answer questions about where he is."

He jerked a thumb back towards the ruined body lying in the spreading pool on the floor.

"Can you do it, ride it out?"

She glanced across the room and shook her head.

"Can I come with you? Will you take me?"

There was no gentleness in his face, he simply nodded at her.

"I'll pick you up later, at the car park. Don't bring too much stuff and don't tell anyone, no-one; do you understand?"

Yet another silent nod was all she could manage. She still shivered, convulsively now and again, but the tears had stopped, dried by the reality of this situation and what it meant to her and to him.

"Now go, don't leave anything here and drive slowly. Go back through the woods, down beside the river, turn right at the fork and that'll see you back to the main road. I'll be in the car park at seven tonight. I'll wait for ten minutes. If you don't come then, I'm gone."

He leaned over towards her and gripped her tight around the top of her arms.

"I like you Sylvie, I'll take you with me if you want to come but you come on my terms, we go where I decide. Okay?"

She nodded at him and then ran to get dressed and pick up her things.

* * *

The car drew away. The headlights flicking through the trees painted a line of green light and then it was gone. Samuel went to the shed and brought back a tarpaulin. He went through the woods, down beside the river, where he disposed of the body.

Now, after his sleep and a shower, he ate some bread torn from a loaf in the cupboard and spread with jam to stave off the hunger and keep his energy levels up. There was just one small moment for something, an emotion, not regret, but an acknowledgement that things had soured again.

Once more his life was being driven by outside forces; he shook his head. That sort of thinking would get him nowhere, it was time to go. He walked around his shack, collecting the few bits he decided he couldn't do without. It wasn't much, this wasn't the first time and in the end one bag and a box of food was all he had to load into the back of the Land Rover.

He went back inside, with a heavy crowbar he smashed at the kitchen units, they'd been fairly new, he had installed them, now they needed to look older. He tore at the mattress and smashed the bath, ripping the shower head from the wall. It would have been best to burn the place but he couldn't risk attracting attention, so this would have to suffice.

He didn't bother to lock the door because he knew he would never come back. Probably someone would come along and occupy it, as he had those few short years ago. Squatters, gypsies, whatever, it didn't matter. If it stayed empty, then, in a surprisingly short time, the woods would obliterate it. The weeds and climbers would swallow it and reduce it so that, eventually only a rusty old sink and the broken stove would be left.

The last thing he did was to open the trap door which had been hidden under the couch. He dragged out a nylon bag, still bulky, still heavy and he tossed it into the back of the car with the rest of the stuff.

He slammed the car door, gunned the engine and left without a backward glance.

Chapter 11

Samuel swung the car into the car park, he didn't look for a space as he didn't intend to stay long. The girl wasn't there. He didn't know how that made him feel.

On the drive from the woods he had acknowledged he didn't need a tag-along, it would be a huge complication. On the other hand, he couldn't be sure what she would do under pressure. What had happened with Phil didn't cause him unease, the scum had been a woman beater, probably a pimp and all that went with it. He was just another low-life and no loss.

Maybe at the end of his life, if he had the time to review the things he had done then this killing would be there, something else to be included in his memories.

The girl though, she had been badly scared. She didn't know him, didn't know anything about him, but she could know enough if anyone asked the right questions. He glanced at his watch. He would go. If she had been intending to come with him she would have been waiting. He leaned to turn the ignition key and caught a shadow moving in his peripheral vision.

She came out from between parked cars, she was wearing jeans and a thick jacket trimmed with fake fur. A pack hung on her back and she carried a holdall. It needed both hands to carry it, her arms were rigid with the strain and it pulled her body sideways, the bulk of it banging against her legs as she staggered across the wet concrete.

He didn't jump out but leaned over and threw open the passenger door. She pushed the bag onto the passenger seat and he hefted it into the rear space. She clambered up and shrugged off the backpack, throwing it into the footwell. One look at her swollen, reddened eyes told him all he needed to know.

He leaned forward, his hands on the top of the steering wheel his forearms resting against the struts. He didn't look at her but just spoke quietly.

"You didn't do anything wrong, Sylvie, you do know that, don't you? He was hurting you and I was the one who killed him. You don't have anything to feel guilty about and you don't have to leave this place if you don't want to. Has anyone asked about him?"

"No, but I didn't go out, I stayed in the flat —couldn't bear to meet anyone."

She turned now, tears were flowing across her cheeks and dripping from her chin. He felt immensely sorry for her and it took him by surprise. It had been many years since he had been visited by the gentler emotions.

"You could just stay here, sit it out. Chances are they won't suspect you had anything to do with it and anyway it could be a long time before they find his body. They don't know yet that anything happened to him. People go away all the time. With someone like him, I think there'll be more relief than regret if he's gone," Samuel said.

"No, no, it won't work, Benny knows, he told him I'd gone with you."

"Ah. Still, you could spin some tale, tell them you only rode with me to the bus station. What did you do with the car?"

"I left it on his street, where he usually parks it. Was that alright? Only you never said what to do with it. I

stuffed the key under the carpet, he does that sometimes –
did, I mean."

"It's fine, good, it'll look normal for a day or two. But
you do know don't you, you don't need to leave this place?
You didn't do anything wrong."

"I want to come with you, Samuel, I want to get away. I
understand if you don't want to take me, but I want to
come with you."

He turned now to look at her, her eyes glistened in the
dim light. She looked like a little girl.

Now the heavy vehicle rumbled across the car park and
out onto the road. Rain had started falling and tiny
starbursts, painted orange by the street lamps, shimmered
on the windscreen.

Sylvie leaned back against the hard seat and for the first
time in this dreadful, desperate day she started to feel safe.

Chapter 12

It was quiet, save for the burble of the diesel and the swish of wet tyres on tarmac. On the few occasions they were overtaken the screen wipers would swish three or four times, clearing the mist of spray. He drove calmly, kept within the speed limits. He was a natural behind the wheel, at one with the car and the road and his situation. Enclosed within this dim little metal cocoon they were divorced from the night and the lives they had fled.

At first Sylvie slumped in the seat, eyes closed and hands idle in her lap. He glanced at her now and again and thought that maybe she was asleep. It was obvious the girl was exhausted, worn out with shock and fear and emotion and he let her be. He preferred the quiet anyway.

After they'd travelled for a while she opened her eyes, like a tired child she simply stayed quite still, limp against the seat. Her head turned slightly to the side as she watched the dark shapes of houses, trees and bigger industrial buildings flicking into being and then slipping away. She had no idea where they were or even which direction they were heading. He had told her they would go where he decided, so she watched as the world slipped past into the night and tried not to think.

He kept away from the motorways. On the very slim chance that all had been discovered, though he doubted it, he steered clear of where the police gathered, the lights were bright and people milled. The car was a gas guzzler and after an hour he refuelled at a small filling station, paying in cash. The pay window for the night-time customers was set low in the wall and he was able to hide most of his face simply by standing erect. There were cameras yes, but he didn't think they needed to worry too much. For most of them the film was cycled every few days and there was no reason to believe they were on anyone's radar yet.

Without speaking Sylvie jumped down and walked into the shop and to the ladies' room in the rear. When she came back she stopped, childlike again, and bought sweets and drinks, a carbonated thing for herself and without asking she bought water for him and filled a small cup of coffee from a machine.

When she clambered back up into the car and handed him the bottle and tiny cardboard cup he smiled at her. She had guessed right, he needed caffeine and rehydration. The gesture and the fact she had known this much so early in their relationship moved him and he leaned over and kissed her cheek.

"Thanks."

She nodded and smiled up shyly. When he had first met her he had taken her for a hard-bitten whore, streetwise and cynical. He thought now, perhaps he'd been wrong.

* * *

For hour after hour they moved along the quiet roads, through estates of houses, windows steamy with condensation, evening meals being prepared, the blue white glow of television screens illuminating small lives. They swept on, past the buses and cars and joggers of suburbia.

She wondered now how he was planning the route, he had no sat nav, she hadn't seen him consult a map and yet he drove on, confident and calm.

He was going north, it was all he needed to know; his sense of direction didn't often fail him and for now at least, simply north was enough. He watched the road signs and knew the country well. In his mind the major towns and the rivers and criss-crossing motorways were an atlas clear enough to lead him in the right direction. Once they got nearer to the coast then he would need to consult the map, probably, but for now he aimed the car towards the pole and drove on.

When the thought struck he was thrown for a moment. He'd been stupid; he was so unnerved by the oversight that he didn't want to ask the question. There was no choice though he would have to ask, and soon, because the answer was pivotal to his plan.

"Sylvie, did you bring your passport?"

"Passport, I don't have a passport."

For a moment he didn't speak, couldn't. It wasn't often that he was so thrown but now for just a little while his mind spiralled uncontrolled. How could she not have a passport, in this day and age, surely everyone had a passport? There were day trips, booze cruises, hen parties, so many things. Now the population looked beyond the shores of Britain for their entertainment, slipped in and out of the country with no thought and little planning.

How could she not have a passport?

He heard the gulp, knew she was barely breathing. She had realised the import of the question and the drama of her response.

"I'm sorry. I never had one, never went anywhere."

"Okay, it's okay, don't worry."

He surprised himself with this need to comfort her; he should let her go. He could leave her at the next big town, give her some money, enough to keep her for a month and then let her find her own way. He was sure that now he had moved her away from the down-at-heel place where she had been born and raised, she probably wouldn't go back. However, she was vulnerable; for all her cockiness when they had first met, she wasn't as streetwise as she thought. If he left her now she would come unstuck. She would probably do what they all do, head for London or Manchester, straight for disaster and a short life of misery and pain.

"It's okay, we can sort it. Don't worry."

The only evidence of his concern, his knuckles white on the wheel, passed her by. She took him at his word and sighed, relaxing back into the seat.

Chapter 13

Eventually Samuel drove into a lay-by beside a dark, two lane road; he turned off the engine.

"I think we should eat something and I need to have a kip."

Sylvie was relieved, she had been drifting in and out of sleep for a while, and she was hungry.

Normally she would have whined about the hunger, bemoaned the endless boring miles and the lack of entertainment but she didn't know this man. Yes, they had enjoyed some sex but more than that, they had seen a man die – had made a man die. She knew nothing more about him than that he could be roused to terrifying physical violence. Her life had been hard and the choices she had made had often been stupid but this situation went beyond anything she could have imagined.

All day she had spent in a haze of indecision and confusion. When she hadn't been curled in a ball on her bed crying she had paced round and round the small living room of the flat. What should she do? Phil was dead, he couldn't come and hurt her, not anymore, and she was honest enough with herself to admit she was glad of it. His mates, Benny and the others didn't frighten her. They were just bullies and big mouths. Without Phil to lead them they wouldn't bother her. She was his girl anyway and until they knew he was gone they wouldn't dare approach her.

That was only part of it though, the easy part, the good part really. She was so very afraid the police would come, that somehow the body had been found, Samuel in custody and her implicated. Every car that slowed outside the window caused her heart to pound and she spent hours peering from behind the curtains, straining to see one way and then the other, sure that at any moment there would be a knock and her life would tumble into the hell she knew prison would be.

Samuel had asked about her parents and she had lied to him then, through shame and because she had lied about them so much she had lost touch with the truth. Her dad had spent most of her childhood in and out of prison. She could remember with shocking clarity her mother screaming at the police cars as they carted him away again and again. He had been a petty criminal, a thug and a loser and when he died in a prison riot she had felt nothing but relief. Her mum had very quickly taken up with another dead loss and that had been the parting of the ways.

Bar work and waitressing, along with what she could draw from Social Services, paid for the crappy little two room flat, and then when Phil came along he had given her the odd hand out. Usually it had to be paid for – carrying packages for him, occasionally having sex with some puffed up old bloke and, of course, with Phil himself.

Thankfully he had liked her enough to keep her mostly to himself, she had never been sure she would have the strength to fight it if he had wanted her to go on the streets, like some of the other girls he ran.

Briefly she had wondered about them, her sisters in torment; who would look out for them now, would they be better or worse off? Some of them would be stuck for drugs without Phil's supply and would have to get out and about on their own. Many would, in the end, be picked up by the police and that in itself presented a risk to her. It was the thought of the police that had made up her mind to pack her stuff and head for the car park and Samuel. He had actually been kind to her and though the fury and the violence when he had killed Phil had shaken her beyond belief, she didn't think he would hurt her.

In truth she liked him, so here she was for the second time in so many days, in the middle of the night, in the middle of nowhere with this man she didn't know. She shook her head in despair. Oh Sylvie where will it all end? A great wave of sadness and hopelessness swept through her and she found she was just too worn out and too tired to care.

"I didn't bring much to eat, Samuel. I had some cheese and a loaf, I put them in here."

She pointed to the pack she had thrown on the floor of the car.

"There's some crisps as well."

"I've got a box, there's a bottle of water and some coffee, I have a stove. We'll be fine. Do you want some coffee?"

"Oh yeah, please. But, well, do you have tea?"

He laughed aloud, it sounded odd to his ears, he hadn't laughed for such a long time and it took him by surprise. He bit it back but it had felt good and he knew there was a smile on his face.

"Yeah, I got tea bags."

She grinned at him now.

"I hope there's milk though, I never could take it without."

"There's milk, it's long life but it's okay. Come on."

They walked to the back of the Land Rover and he opened the rear doors. A box stowed under the rear seat held a small camping stove, a tin kettle with a folding handle and an enamel mug. He rooted around in the bottom for a while and came up with a plastic cup, he peered inside, poured a drop of water into it, swilled it round and then wiped it on a piece of paper towel.

Once the stove was lit, standing on the kerb edge and the water was hissing and singing, he dragged out the cardboard box he had packed back at the shack. He had pretty much emptied the kitchen cupboard into it. They made sandwiches with tinned ham and cheese slices, he brewed tea for her and coffee for himself and they sat on the back seat of the car so they could put the food between them.

For a while they ate in silence, worn down by the travelling and the things that had brought them here, and each lost in thoughts they couldn't share and didn't know what to do with.

It was peaceful though; it was calm and there was a gentle companionship between them the like of which Sylvie had never known and Samuel had thought he would never experience again.

She knew that before long it would all need to come out, her life with Phil, the truth about her mum and dad and then he'd probably dump her, and she wouldn't blame him. For now it was enough to sit in the dark and the quiet, to sip the warm tea and watch the dark shadow of Samuel outlined against the rain-specked window.

Chapter 14

After the food they settled down in the darkness, Samuel stretched across the rear seat, as much as the confined space would allow, and Sylvie curled in the front, covered with her coat. It was cosy with only the distant swish of cars on the road and the patter of the rain on the roof.

When Sylvie opened her eyes it was still dark but the sky was paler and she guessed it must be almost dawn. Samuel was outside, the little stove was lit and the kettle was on, he was using a torch to find his way around. She pushed open the door and jumped out into the damp and dreary morning.

"Alright?" he asked.

"Mm, I slept well, surprised myself really. Did you?"

"Yes, no problem, I'm used to dossing down here and there."

It was the first time he had given any sort of information about his life and she waited to see if he would continue, but he turned back to the rear of the car where he had opened the food box. He dragged out a box of biscuits and offered her one.

"I think we can go for some breakfast in a little while, so this is just a good morning sugar treat."

"Thanks. Will it be okay? Safe, I mean."

"Oh, I think so, the best thing we can do is just act normal. Nobody here has any reason to look at us twice. Even when his mates find Phil is missing, and it shouldn't be for a while yet, I don't believe it will cause us any problems. A low-life like him, they disappear, nobody cares, some people just breathe a sigh of relief and everyone carries on. Did he have family, do you know?"

She shook her head, she wasn't ready, not yet, oh please not yet. Later today, she would tell him about herself, but when she had seen him, through the car window, she had felt such a rush of warmth and she didn't want to spoil it.

She shivered in the damp air and Samuel walked to the front of the Land Rover and dragged her jacket out, it still held some of the night warmth and he draped it around her shoulders. She needed to pee and she needed to clean her teeth. It was time to stop being so wimpy.

"I'm going in the bushes for a mo."

He reached into the box and brought out a roll of kitchen towel. She stared at him for a minute and then with a little giggle, part embarrassment, part genuine amusement, she tore off a piece and fought her way through the shrubs bordering the lay-by.

While she was gone he'd packed up the stove, but her cup was still there, steam rising into the damp morning and she cupped her hands around the heat. He had made them coffee and added milk and sugar, she didn't normally add sugar but the sweetness was comforting.

"We can drive into town this morning, for breakfast. If we pick a fast food place we'll be able to use their bathrooms for a quick wash and stuff. Okay?"

She nodded at him. He was so very different from the way she thought he would be. His size was intimidating and his previous surly manner had been a bit scary. In the bar when she had first decided to approach him, she had been a little afraid but the thought of easy money had made her brave. Now though, on this dim, quiet morning she saw a big man with a kind manner. His thick, brown hair was touched with a little grey and his face was rugged and weather-worn. A shadow of stubble hinted at the beard that would grow were he to give it a chance and above it the dark blue eyes twinkled now and again as the moisture glinted in a stray gleam of light from passing cars or his torch.

He had a calmness about him that was comforting and she detected nothing but friendship in the way he was treating her. How could it be? She had gone to hell and back in his presence and yet he was behaving as if they were on any old road trip, almost a holiday.

He turned to her and as their eyes met, something, a frisson, a connection passed between them. She had to turn away and her hands had begun to shake. She gulped back the last of her cooling coffee and then wiped out the plastic cup with more of the kitchen roll.

He packed away the last of their stuff, slammed the back door and climbed into the driving seat. Sylvie was still shaken, she was sure that in his eyes, she had seen something: a glimpse of feeling, just a hint of softening and maybe even of desire.

She told herself it was the circumstances, nothing more than a male-female interaction. She knew she wasn't bad looking and was used to blokes coming on to her, but him, now? She shook her head slightly, she couldn't deal with any more complications right now and there was still the difficult conversation facing her. Once they had it, then probably the parting of the ways would come very quickly. She slid into the car and closed her eyes as the vehicle nosed its way back onto the main road and headed for the town.

Chapter 15

"Samuel, can I explain about Phil? I don't know what you think, thought, about us – him and me."

"You told me he was your boyfriend, I saw a thug beating you up. I think you should pick better boyfriends. You don't need to tell me anything. Your life is your concern."

The sharpness of the answer brought tears to her eyes and for a moment she simply sat quietly, willing them not to roll down her face. She didn't want him to know he could upset her so easily. After a minute she cleared her throat and started speaking again.

"He wasn't my pimp, I suppose you think that."

She saw he was about to speak and raised a hand to still him.

"We got it on now and again and he gave me money, but he didn't make me turn tricks, well not regularly. He did with quite a few girls. The ones he supplied with drugs were stuck with it but not me. Now and again there were friends." She let it go now, she heard what she was saying and saw it for what it was, feeble excuses for things that shamed her.

Samuel shook his head but now she had started, it had become vital that he understood.

"I was just getting by, in the flat and I met him and we liked each other, well I liked him, whether he did or not, I don't know. Anyway for a while it was good, then he made me do things I didn't want to. I decided to get out so he started to hit me. For the last year I've tried over and over to get rid of him but it was impossible."

"Why didn't you go and stay with your mum and dad?"

She took in a great breath and sighed.

"I couldn't, my dad's dead and I don't know where Mum is, don't care, don't want to know."

"You said they moved to be near your gran."

"I lied. My dad was a no-good loser and my mum was hopeless. I'm ashamed of them and I never tell people about them, the lies just come out. I said stuff like that about them for so long now it feels like the truth. My dad died in jail. I'm not like that though, I'm not, Samuel. I know you probably think I was on the game but I'm not. Okay I did think I could try and lift some stuff from your house. Everyone seemed to think you were rich and I thought if I gave you a good time then I could just take some stuff and it would be fair. I didn't though. I wouldn't. Once I had spent some time with you – you know, at your place – I wouldn't have taken anything. I liked you, I like you."

By now she was sniffing and the tears which had been beaten back earlier had breached her defences and she was wiping her streaming eyes on the sleeve of her thin sweatshirt. He reached over and flipped the rag from the dashboard onto her lap.

"Okay."

As he spoke she turned and looked up at him, her eyes alight with tears and hope and fear. It broke him up inside to see such raw emotion.

"Look, I would have given you some money and don't really care what you intended to do. It all went down a different way, anyway. I don't want to know about your parents, I know already what Phil was like, just don't tell me any more and don't tell me any lies. Okay?"

She sniffed loudly, rubbed at her face with the piece of cloth and again turned to him.

"You're not going to dump me are you, Samuel? Please. I don't know what I'll do now."

"No, I'm not going to do that but no more lies. No more stories about your past. It's just that, *yours*, I don't want it."

"Okay."

He had turned into the car park of a McDonalds and as they strode quickly towards the golden arches and the bright, greasy world of junk food and normality she almost skipped. She had told him and he hadn't thrown her out. For now it was enough.

They sat together on tall stools by the window and watched the day begin. No-one gave them a second glance and for a brief spell they existed in the same normal, humdrum world as the rest of humanity.

Just before they began gathering the garbage and sliding their feet from the stools onto the greasy floor she reached and took his hand, squeezing his fingers.

"Thank you, Samuel."

He nodded, just once, and then turned from her to head for the men's room and a quick wash. She followed and turned into the women's toilets where she did what she could with the liquid soap and the bits and pieces of toiletries in her handbag. She felt better but wondered how long it would be before she could have a shower and change her things.

They met back outside and in moments were on the road. She felt a difference in his driving, he was more direct and more specific about the roads he followed. It seemed now he had a destination in mind. Something had happened yesterday to change his plans but she couldn't think what it might be and in truth all she wanted to do now was hand over her future and simply be.

Chapter 16

They shopped at a huge supermarket just off the motorway and took the opportunity to buy a meal in the little cafe. It was dull, badly cooked and tasteless but it filled their bellies and gave them the energy to keep going. Sylvie had wondered if they were going to share the driving but he simply kept on and on, covering the miles. They chatted now and again about incidentals on the route, but mostly they were quiet.

She was desperate to know where they were heading but he had made it plain from the very beginning that he was travelling and she was along simply because he allowed her to be. She'd packed her iPod in the bag which was unreachable in the back, and anyway she didn't think she could just sit and listen to music with Samuel beside her quiet and focused on the driving. The old car had a radio but he had made no move to turn it on, so she had assumed it was broken or simply that he wanted quiet. She gave him quiet.

At times though, during the day she found the atmosphere and her dark memories oppressive; twice she tried to talk about Phil. She thought she needed to know what happened to him, to his body, after she had fled in quivering panic through the early morning. Twice her words were stilled by a glance from the man beside her and a shake of his head. He spoke of it briefly, just once.

"I dealt with it, it's done. Now, all we can do is wait and hope and the longer we wait the better it will be, so you need to push it to the back of your mind. Don't let it rule you."

Now and again they would try to break the uneasy silence but it was strained and perfunctory. So many miles together in the little cab for two virtual strangers could be difficult in any case, but with the horrific and tormented beginning to their relationship it seemed impossible to get things onto an even keel. Like a great spectre between them, the memory of the sex and then the violence and the fact that they had seen the best and the worst of each other in quick succession had built a wall impossible to scale.

As the day drew on the dullness and monotony was soporific and Sylvie let her thoughts drift. She was in a doze for a lot of the time, lulled by the sound of the engine and the rocking of the big car. She was jolted from her half-dream as Samuel muttered to her.

"We're nearly there now."

The bald statement caused her stomach to flip with excitement. They had passed through the Midlands and into Lancashire; she had picked up clues in the road signs. Crewe, Nantwich –they were in Cheshire. Soon afterwards they skirted the great spread of the city of Liverpool. They stopped on the outskirts of Preston and had a cup of coffee and toasted buns at a roadside stall. From across the fields she had a glimpse of the cupola on the buildings of the University of Lancaster. She was surprised; her expectations of the north had been dirty towns, mean streets and factories. In reality though there was green everywhere, neat little villages and signs of affluence, especially as they'd driven through Cheshire.

They drove around the flat sweep of Morecambe Bay with its deadly sands and murderous tides and in the background, against the great grey sweep of cloud, were the blue-green hills of The Lakes.

It was gorgeous, there was water everywhere: rills, and rivers, streams and of course lakes. The winding roads meandered through little gatherings of houses, painted cottages with slate roofs and mile after mile of stone walling. Undulating fells and dales were scattered with grubby sheep and at times they would round a corner and the view of stream, cliff, lake and woodland would simply take her breath away. She'd had no idea it was so beautiful in this northern part of her own country and the wonder of it all expunged for this brief time the misery of the last few days and the worry about what would come next.

The high, wide sky was grey scudding cloud until every now and again the sun would force a few beams through to spotlight a cliff top or a sparkling, dancing stretch of water. She was mesmerised.

They passed Windermere and then after another half hour or so wound down a narrow, one lane road between cottages with bright painted doors that opened directly onto the street. Samuel was unhesitating, it was obvious he was familiar with the area and knew exactly where he was heading.

He swung the car carefully around a tight bend, pulled into the side and then reached into the back of the car. He dragged out his waterproof jacket and shrugged it over his shoulders. It was difficult in the confined space and she helped him, holding the sleeve so he could slide his arm into it. She expected that he would jump down, perhaps he needed to pee. Once he had the coat on though he just shrugged up the hood, pulling it forward over his face. He drew back onto the road and drove a few minutes towards the borders of the little hamlet. Almost at the edge of the village there were a few modern houses stood back from the road in simple gardens. He reversed up a narrow lane and then turned off the car engine and sat for a moment watching through the window into the gathering dusk. When he was satisfied, with what she wasn't sure, he clicked open the door.

"Hang on here for a bit. If you see anyone coming just keep your head down. I won't be long."

She nodded and watched him walk back the way they had just driven. The evening air quickly chilled the interior of the car and she dragged her own jacket over the seat back and shuffled herself into it. The engine ticked and clicked as it cooled and the evening song of birds she couldn't name were the only other company. She waited, her nerves jangled and her mind racing as she tried to guess just what was happening now. She had handed her living over to this man totally in the last two days and she felt adrift, floating unconnected, part of it was a peaceful feeling, like a child letting others make the decisions. There was also the reality of worry and fear about yet another ill thought out situation in her tumbled and chaotic young life.

Chapter 17

The beam of a torch swung through the darkness picking out the gnarled and tormented branches of hedgerows and Sylvie bobbed her head down below the level of the dashboard. It was Samuel, he swung the door open.

"Okay, it's a little walk, you take the smaller bags."

While Sylvie climbed down onto the mud of the turn-in he opened the rear doors and retrieved the bags and laid them on the ground. She reached for her own and the smaller one of his.

"Hold on, I need to pull the car further back."

He slid behind the wheel and reversed until the car could barely be seen through the overhanging branches and tall weeds.

"That'll have to do for tonight. Come on, can you manage those bags?"

She bent and lifted them one in each hand, but he had already turned away to retrieve the remaining holdalls.

"I'll come for the food box later."

He strode off glancing behind just once to check if she was managing to keep up, laden as she was with the two bags and her rucksack swinging from one shoulder.

They walked for a couple of minutes. Up ahead, the door of one of the small cottages opened and a spill of yellow light fell onto the narrow pathway and across the road. Samuel drew back into the hedgerow pulling her with him and throwing a hand across the front of her to hold her still on the uneven ground. She hardly dared to breathe, though in truth she had no idea what this was all about. She knew neither where they were going nor who they were hiding from specifically. He had shown no concern in the McDonalds or the supermarket so why now, in the dusky light of the Lake District evening, was he so nervous and secretive? A figure emerged from the little house and turned to walk off in the other direction from them. The burning ashes of a discarded cigarette end sparkled like a tiny firework and then were extinguished in the night. The silhouette faded becoming vague and insubstantial as it moved off into the darkness.

When he was happy there was no-one else around, they drew forward again into the drive of the last of the houses. He led her down the small stretch of concrete and pushed open the front door. It was cold and clammy inside and although it didn't smell of neglect and dirt it had obviously been shut up for some time. The air was still and stale. There was the faint smell of bathroom cleaner and an air freshener had been left somewhere imbuing the atmosphere with an artificial chemical scent.

He pushed the door closed and dropped the luggage.

"I'm sorry we can't put any lights on, but once your eyes adjust I think you'll manage. I can't turn the heating on, the steam from the vent might be seen from outside. Are you okay, Sylvie?"

His tone was gentle now and he placed his hands on her upper arms rubbing up and down as if he were trying to warm her. His manner had changed, as if he had reached a sanctuary and could let go the grip on his nerves.

"You've been very patient and I know I haven't been any company but I wanted to get us somewhere safe. I don't think we have any need to worry but I don't like it when I'm not in control. I was heading for Hull, planning on Holland, but you having no passport, it threw me. It's okay, it's okay," he said.

"It's not your fault, you didn't know and I can sort it, but it'll take a few days and I didn't want to risk hotels and so on, just in case. We should be okay here though, but it's essential no-one knows, so we'll keep the lights out. The cooker is gas and has an external vent so it's a no go, I'll bring the camping stove and we can make a drink and a sandwich," he continued.

"Tomorrow I'll get things sorted better but let's just be careful for now okay?"

The small physical contact had almost reduced her to tears and she couldn't speak but gave him a quivering smile. When he looked down at her, his eyes were gentle and the hard lines of his face softened. He was somehow more human.

"I know I've said this before, but you know you aren't in any trouble, Sylvie, you didn't do anything wrong. If all this is too much for you, and I wouldn't blame you if it was, then I can take you to Windermere tomorrow. You can get a train to Manchester and on to wherever you like. I have to get out of the country at least for a while but you don't."

"I'd rather stay with you, Samuel. I would never tell anyone about what happened I want you to know that, never, ever, but I just feel so lost right now and I don't know what I'd do if you weren't here. Yes, I'd rather stay with you. I'm sorry about the passport."

He shook his head.

"No, we can stay here for a few days and then we can probably carry on."

He glanced round in the darkness and she detected a slump in his shoulders as he turned his head, taking in what could be seen of the small lounge and the kitchen beyond.

"I thought a passport took weeks and cost a load of money. I haven't got much money."

"It's okay, we can't go down the usual route now anyway, don't worry, I know some people."

"Where is this place, Samuel? Is it a holiday cottage? I saw there were loads of them all around. I'm not surprised, it's lovely up here, I had no idea how nice it was."

"Yes it is lovely and no, this isn't a holiday cottage, this is mine, this is my home."

Chapter 18

Holding the torch low, he led her to the stairs. They had scratched together an evening meal from the things picked up at the supermarket. With the small stove screened behind the open kitchen door, they had made tea. Pulling cups and plates from the cupboards and dusting them quickly on a towel he had revealed a domesticated side that argued with the ramshackle, dragged together man she had spent time with in the shack.

The travelling and the stress had worn them down and, as soon as they had finished their food, they left the dirty pots in the sink and made their way upstairs. He was confident and unhesitating walking around in the dark, he knew this house well.

It was strange to see him now. Sylvie had only ever been aware of him as the weirdo in the woods but watching him here it was difficult to believe he hadn't spent all his time here, in this little place in the Lake District. She was confused and longed to question him.

The small landing with four doors lined along one wall was reached by an open wooden staircase. He threw open the first of the doors.

"Bathroom."

She nodded, assuming there would be no hot water but at least she could have a good wash. He surprised her yet again with his intuition.

"I've turned on the electric. I think that, providing you leave the room light off and don't open the window, you can have a shower; it's an instant heat thing, but use your own towel. We have to be careful, when we leave here it must look as though we've never been. I have someone come in about once a month to check it all out and to clean, I'm not sure when they are next due. I don't want there to be any sort of trail, just on the off-chance that anyone asks questions.

He pushed the next door, the curtains were open and the moonlight through the little window outlined a bed and dresser. The floor was covered with a light-coloured carpet, this house was homely and comfortable.

"You can sleep in here if you want. Strip the bed though, we'll use the blankets from the car. I know it's not as comfortable but again I don't want to leave evidence. Tomorrow we could pick up some cheap sheets and then take them with us when we go. Will you be warm enough?"

It was a pivotal moment, Sylvie understood and she weighed her options.

"Maybe it would be warmer if we shared the blankets."

She didn't want him to turn her down, couldn't bear it if he rejected her now. She felt sad and vulnerable and the thought of lying in the cold and the dark of this small room was horrible. She wanted to curl up with this big bear of a man who had, to her amazement, proved to be a gentle, caring person. She wanted him to be a friend, and life had instructed her that the way to achieve friendship with a man was to offer her body.

He stood before her, his head cocked to one side and then with a brief nod he turned and entered the room.

"We'll use this room. I'll go and get the blankets. You can have a shower now if you want to but leave the light off, can you manage?"

"Yes. Thanks Samuel."

The shower was wonderful, and as she rubbed cream into her warmed skin and slipped into a clean T-shirt for sleeping, she felt relaxed and there was a tiny germ of happiness uncurling in her heart. If only this could have really been a holiday. She had never had one and this was exactly what she would have wished for, a sweet little house, a different environment and a kind friend.

She heard the door click quietly and held her breath for a moment until she realised that the chance of it being any other than Samuel was so remote as to be impossible. As she went back into the bedroom he had begun to strip off his travel-stained, stale clothes. She crossed the carpet and wrapped her arms around his naked upper body. As he hugged her in return she laid her head against the strength of his chest and in the dark and the silence she heard the muted thudding of his heart.

Chapter 19

It was raining in the Lake District, as it was across the whole of the country. Rain had fallen unrelentingly in southern parts for two days. The dancing droplets had peppered the slow sweep of the river and dribbled from the leaves of the old trees. The soil had sucked it in.

The willow had stood for more than a century, perched on the banks of the river. Rain from the streaming branches dripped endlessly into little runnels formed around the base and trickled away to join the rising flow. Mud slid down the incline and as the level rose the homes of the rats and voles were flooded and the grass of the banks was swallowed by the swelling waters.

Further north, Samuel and Sylvie had spent the night curled together under the inadequate covering. While he had taken a quick shower she had lain under the woollen blankets, cold and a little apprehensive. She was experienced sexually, able to satisfy animal lust with men like Phil, but she had never made love to anyone. Now, with Samuel her heart craved affection, and tenderness.

He climbed in beside her bringing the damp warmth of the bathroom with him. He still hadn't shaved and the rough stubble was harsh against her cheek as she turned to him, it was real and honest and she revelled in the masculinity of it. He kissed her. The last time, in the shack, there had been no kissing though the sex had been kind; now his warm lips pressed gently onto hers and she opened her mouth in response.

His hands explored her warming body, hesitant at first, still testing, asking questions which she answered with moves of her own. As his confidence grew and the memory of passion came back to him, he caressed her breasts, her thighs and her belly. As they discovered each other the growing sensations took her away, from the worry and the fear and stress. Her dark world filled with pleasure and, at the end, the nearest thing to ecstasy she had ever known.

For Samuel it was a revelation, he had been convinced for years that the only sexual release he would have would be of his own making. It had become nothing more than a physical necessity. It left him saddened and bereft reminding him as it did of what had been and what he truly believed was no longer for him.

This young body, supple and giving in the darkness, dragged him back to a place he had lost and, though he never for one moment forgot this was Sylvie, it didn't feel like the betrayal he had always imagined. As the sex became something deeper and more spiritual he believed he felt a benediction, it was right it should be here in this place that had once meant so much and, against everything he would have imagined, he felt no guilt. With Sylvie totally in the ultimate moments, he felt the great shift of grief and his soul soared and his life began again.

They woke early to the gentle sound of the rain on the window panes and, though they knew the day would hold challenges to be met, they gifted themselves the time to endorse their new relationship, loving each other once more in the grey morning as they had in the darkness.

Chapter 20

"We have to be very careful, it's important that the house looks empty and when we leave there's no trace of us ever having been here. I have to go out soon, there's no signal here for a mobile phone or my internet dongle. You can come with me if you like or you can stay in here, it's up to you. If you do stay, keep away from the windows and try not to disturb things too much."

"It's okay, Samuel, I'll stay here if you don't mind and I'll be careful. I know I've been a bit of a wimp up to now but, really I'm fine. I can look after myself normally, well, much better than you probably think," Sylvie replied.

"This is a lovely house, I don't understand why you'd want to be living in the woods, down south, in an awful shack, when you've got this," she continued.

"There's things you don't know, Sylvie, there's reasons I can't be here."

He looked down at her, tumbled and warmed by their morning passion and he let his heart feel the pleasure, it was good. Sitting back down on the side of the bed he took hold of her hand.

"Look, there's stuff I need to tell you. It's only fair, and afterwards you have to make a decision about what you want to do. I won't try to influence you and I'll respect any decision you make, but let me do this stuff first. We need to be ready, to get everything sorted out and carry on with the plan to get out of the country, for a while at least. Come on, get yourself dressed. I'll go and put the kettle on."

She dressed and plodded down the stairs to find Samuel inexplicably taking photographs with a digital camera. The toaster, the kettle and the dishes in the cupboards. He heard her come to stand beside him and grinned at her puzzled expression.

"No, I'm not losing it. I thought if I took pictures we can make sure we put all the stuff back in the same place before we leave. It'll mean we can relax a bit more. Now, get your drink and I made some toast, there's jam," he said.

He continued, "We need to take a photograph for your passport. It would be really good if we could change the way you look a bit, but there isn't time for much. You need to look just a bit different, but not enough so you feel awkward, because you need to be relaxed for going through customs."

"I can do that."

She grabbed her hot drink and skipped back up the stairs where he could hear her dragging her bag across the floor and then the bathroom door opened.

He stood gazing out of the kitchen window. It was all still the same, unchanging and ignorant of the rough tides which had driven through his life. The memories were still so strong, all the dreams and the days and the loving and the laughter.

"Ta da!"

He spun round. She had sprayed some dark red colour into her blond hair, streaks of it along her fringe and in strands here and there. She had then pulled it back and piled it high on her head. The difference was surprising, her eyes looked larger and her neck, bare now, was long and elegant. She had a tiny glittering stud above her top lip and along her ears were rows of gold coloured hoops that followed the curve to the very top. She had applied kohl makeup to her eyes quite heavily and had painted a small beauty spot high on her cheek. Her lips were dark red and fuller now with the effect of the cosmetics.

She was a lovely looking girl, striking as she stood before him now like this with the jewels and the war paint but he preferred her as she had been just a short hour ago, flushed with sleep and blurry with passion in his bed.

He shook his head, the difference was astounding. "How, did you do that?"

"This is the other me." She giggled at the look on his face.

"I didn't see, you know all those holes in your ears."

"No, I don't wear the rings much anymore but the holes are still there. Actually I had a bit of a struggle with some of them and I think they're going to be sore but not so bad."

"Well, it's perfect. Just different enough and with all the metal work…" He pointed at her grinning face. "…You give people things to think about, it's the best sort of disguise. Stand over there by the wall. I have a setting on this camera for ID pictures. You're not allowed to smile."

"Okay."

The job was done quickly, he took several pictures. "I might need to get these printed, I can go to a supermarket while I'm out, I'll see what I need. Are you going to be okay here on your own?"

"Yes, I'll be fine."

She took the few steps towards him and held out her hand.

"Samuel, about last night. Well, last night and this morning; thank you."

In response he simply wrapped his big arms around her and drew her to him.

"No, Sylvie, no. Thank you."

As she backed away she saw the glitter of tears on his dark lashes and she ducked her head so he couldn't see she too was overwhelmed.

For a while, after Samuel left on his quest for a phone signal and onward from wherever that had led, Sylvie played house. She repacked the clothes in her bag; at first she was afraid to use the iron and ironing board but it was simply stored in a corner of the kitchen and she was sure she could return it so that it would appear undisturbed.

She pressed the creases out of her trousers and shirts and hung them on the empty hangers in the bedroom wardrobe. It would have been fun to display her toiletries in the bright bathroom but she didn't want Samuel to think she had taken liberties. His kindness, his passion and the growing affection between them was precious and she didn't want to risk upsetting him. Until she knew him better she was willing to move slowly and cautiously if it meant it would keep her with him.

She lay on the bed for a while listening to her iPod but none of the stored music suited her mood. She wavered between thrill at the events of the night and morning and residual misery at the memory of what had brought them here. She turned to the radio trying to find a station to entertain and relax her but was dissatisfied with them all. It struck her then that she hadn't had any real contact with the outside world for a couple of days now, confined to the car and now here in this place devoid of internet and without a television.

She listened to the news, fearing every item, praying silently that there would be no mention of Phil and his disappearance. She still had no idea what Samuel had done with the body and it seemed he wasn't willing to share any information. In truth she was happier that way, could more easily turn from the pictures filling her mind if the story wasn't finished. There was a tiny nugget of fear eating away continually in the back of her mind. If his body was found, she assumed her own disappearance would be noted and a search for her would follow.

There was nothing though, and when the weather report began with news of torrential rain covering practically the whole of the country she turned off the radio with a sigh of relief.

Back in the kitchen she made a drink and a sandwich. Samuel had given her no idea of how long he might be away and, unable to stray outdoors and with the strict constraint on her movements inside the house, she grew restless and bored. She knew now that actually she would have been better going with Samuel in the car.

She wandered back to the bedroom but found nothing to do. An idea slid through her mind briefly but she didn't believe Samuel would appreciate her unpacking or ironing his clothes. She pulled her own bag to the corner of the room, allowing easier access to the dresser, she dragged his nearer to the wall to make a wider space beside the bed. There were two bags, a small one which was gaping open to reveal his clothes and toiletries and the large black hold-all which he had carried from the car. She was amazed by the weight of it as she struggled to drag it across the carpet and push it, bulky and intriguing, alongside its mate.

The honourable thing obviously was to leave it closed and she was determined to respect his privacy but the temptation to pry was enormous. She left the room closing the door on the tantalising piece of luggage and turned to the stairs. Out of sight, out of mind she hoped.

Boredom and inactivity played its part and natural inquisitiveness drew her back to the other doors on the landing. He hadn't said she couldn't have free access to the whole house. He had simply said she must keep away from the windows and outside doors and not use any heating lest the steam from the vent was seen outside. She laid her hand on the handle, for a moment she was undecided, was it moral to explore? She couldn't imagine why it would not be so she turned the knob and pushed against the wood.

The door swung back to reveal another room with the curtains open letting in the rain-soaked light of the late morning. The walls were palest yellow and half way down was a border of cartoon animals and colourful alphabet letters. On the wall opposite the window great cartoon sheep gambolled across bright green hillsides peppered with yellow flowers. Against the wall behind the door stood a white cot, a changing table flanked one side and a tiny bassinet on a wooden stand was placed at the bottom. There was a tall chest which had been painted in pale pastels and decorated with cartoon decals.

Sylvie's hands flew to her mouth.

Chapter 21

She moved further into the little room, it was clean but the atmosphere was closed up and suspended. There were no fluffy blankets on the cot, no tiny teddy bear propped in the corner of the bassinet and no tinkling, glittering mobile dangling from the ceiling hook. A display in a department store would hold more life.

The surfaces were bare, covered with a thin layer of dust as had been the rest of the house. The cleaner must be due to come soon. She slid open the first three drawers of the dresser, there were no cute miniature outfits or soft sheets and coverlets. This nursery was waiting, for a tiny inhabitant, for the smell of milk and baby powder and the sound of lullabies. The rocking chair in the corner was forlorn in its stillness, the room would have been better picked up and packed away, so great was the air of abandonment.

She dragged open the lowest drawer, there was a flat packet lying on the bottom and she reached in and lifted it out. It was obvious immediately that it was a frame, wrapped in a piece of towelling.

She placed the parcel onto the top of the dresser, her hands were shaking and there was a risk it would be dropped and damaged. She unfolded the soft fabric. In the bright picture a young, dark haired woman, in the early stages of pregnancy smiled out at her. She was leaning into the arms of a tall man in military uniform. The soldier held her lovingly around her waist, big hands spread over the slightly swollen belly. Samuel cradling his unborn child.

The discovery of this sad space had been so surprising that her nerves felt jolted. Samuel must be married, or at some time he had been, or anyway there had been a partner. His past was a secret place and there had been no reason for her to make assumptions but she had never imagined him with a family. The reality of him with a baby was impossible to equate with the surly and brusque person she had first met. True, the Samuel emerging now was very different but, a family man, a daddy, she was completely unprepared for this.

The love captured by the camera was real and undeniable. Where were they now, this lovely woman and the child she had carried? How had this love been lost and what misery had resulted in this empty, forlorn little room, and was it the reason Samuel had been hiding in the forest so many miles away?

None of it made sense, he was older than she was, but surely he wasn't so old that his military career had reached its end. What was he hiding from, why was he running? She had known from the very start that he was on the outside limit of society but now layer upon layer of mystery was building and it left her bemused and uneasy.

She wrapped the picture carefully and replaced it, sliding the drawer home. Backing out of the little room she took one last look before closing the door as gently as if a child slumbered in the white cot. The pleasure she had taken from this little house felt flattened now and she went back into the bedroom and flopped onto the bed.

She tried to think rationally; so he was married, or he had been. There was nothing unusual in a broken marriage, no surprise in a fractured family – it meant very little these days. What if the photograph had captured a time of love and happiness? So did millions of wedding portraits: times changed, people fell out of love and moved on. Did it explain why the nursery was still there, yet not quite there, a shadow of what it should have been? Where were the bits and pieces left after a sharp and sorrowful split, the old outfits, no longer worth packing and carrying away, where were the half empty bottles and jars? Maybe it had been so long ago that those things had been discarded, but if so why not the rest of it? Surely the cartoon characters should have been swamped below a coat of bland emulsion and the furniture replaced by a bed or perhaps equipment for an older child, visiting for a weekend with daddy. This wasn't normal, not in her understanding of human behaviour, limited though she knew this to be. It was odd.

She swivelled her head on the bare mattress, there in the corner was the big black bag. She didn't think about it now, there was no internal struggle, sliding from the bed she took two small steps, bent and pulled the zip.

The bag gaped open, filled as it was almost to the top. She reached in and dragged out one of the bundles. How much was this? She could not compute the amount; she had never imagined she would ever see so much money in one place at one time. She plunged her hands in further and drew another wad from the bottom, there must be thousands and thousands of pounds here, all neatly bundled and all high denomination notes. The fear now was real and sparking on her nerve endings; this was wrong, there couldn't be a simple explanation. The rumours had been true, he was rich, he had a great holdall full of money, her heart pounded as she looked at it, not with avarice, but with an animal instinct to flee and an acknowledgement that this could be the means.

Chapter 22

Samuel had driven out of the valley to find a strong signal for his phone. He would need to pull in favours. Contact with the people from before was something he had managed to avoid for the past three years, but it was his best option now. He had really hoped it was over, though in honesty acknowledged it might never be. This favour would have to be paid for with one in return and he would be swept back into the maelstrom he had fought to escape. He shrugged and focused, there was no point grieving – this had to be done.

He should have a passport for Sylvie in a day or two and then they could carry on.

He struggled with the concept of them as a couple. For many years he had been alone, through choice and necessity, and he was sorely afraid it was best to keep it so. It wasn't fair to form a relationship with this young woman. It was too risky letting the attraction grow into something stronger, letting down his guard and starting to believe. It had all gone so horribly wrong before and the dangers in his life now were even greater.

For a moment the memory of his other love overwhelmed him, a painful twist in his gut. He knew it of old, faced it and rode it out – the desolation that had gripped him for so long, was always but a small beat away. He would never again feel complete, his heart had been ripped out and the void was a part of him real and permanent forever.

Yes, these last two days with Sylvie had been good, really good. Last night had shown him he could still find pleasure and gentleness and passion, but he wasn't ready to try to heal, he didn't want to. The person he had once been was a stranger, lost in the murk behind all the things he had done since then; unreachable. This entity that he had become was broken and ruined, undeserving of happiness.

He would take her with him to Holland and then when they were sure it was safe, he would send her back. He would give her money and advice and make her accept her freedom. It was the right thing to do and for once he was going to do the right thing.

He made his calls, organised things, emailed the digital images. He bought milk and bread from a tiny shop attached to a filling station. Then he turned to the winding road that would take him back to the place which had once formed the whole of his world.

* * *

In the south, the river continued to swell with the torrential rain; the wind was building now and great branches whipped and groaned. It was many years since the level had reached so high on the ancient banks. Small rocks and boulders began to break away and tumble into it. The smaller shrubs and bushes held out until the soil beneath their roots was eroded and then they in turn joined the detritus flowing seaward. At times debris from the banks would catch and wedge against a barrier of mud and green stuff until the bulk of it formed a whole which was too big to hold and then, jolted by a greater clump, it flushed downstream.

The branches of the willow flicked and whipped in the gusts, the trunk bent and groaned with the strain and the great roots pulled and dragged at the mud of the new formed river bank. Holes were fashioned beneath the old tree, the water crept further into the darkness, flowing around the rocks and boulders and creeping between the decaying limbs of the soaking corpse.

* * *

In the cottage Sylvie curled into a ball on the couch in the living room, she had cried a little and then acknowledged she had no right to tears. What Samuel was, what he had done was no concern of hers, and his past was his alone.

She had chosen, for poor and squalid reasons, to approach him and through that she had drawn him into this nightmare. The money, the sorry little nursery and this place were not hers and the proper, honest thing for her to do would be to leave. He had a right to his life no matter what misery or joy it may hold and there was no reason to believe there was space for her within it.

She could take some of the money, she didn't want to but saw no other choice. There were so many bundles; a few notes from each one would be unnoticed. Though she didn't know really where they were or how to get away, she wasn't stupid. Even in this day and age she had hitched at times and once she was in a decent sized town there would be buses, trains, the whole of the transport system. With some money she could go anywhere and sort herself out.

The ghost of his arms around her, the memory of his body against hers and the rush of love she felt for him were the cause of her tears and the root of the struggle pinning her now to this room and this house.

* * *

Back on the road Samuel glanced again into his rear-view mirror. On a wet Lakeland evening the roads were relatively quiet, he was probably being paranoid. He had kept the phone calls short and discarded the SIM quickly, but the black Range Rover he had noticed outside the garage was still there now. After each bend and turn in the road it shadowed his route. His instinct for self-preservation didn't like it, not one bit.

Chapter 23

He had been gone a long time, the light was fading and the rain was heavier now. She had thought he would be away just a few hours, back long ago, and she felt sharp regret at the decision to wait in the house. Fear shot through her; what if he'd left her, abandoned to whatever came, and even now was boarding the ferry to Holland or driving through the night somewhere else?

Her head and her heart had argued all day, she wanted to flee, just go and find somewhere to rest and recover, to be alone and find some quiet. A greater part of her wanted to stay and wait for him. More than anything else she wanted to be with Samuel. The need to speak to him was a physical ache, there was a desperate wish to ask him to explain, if he would, and her hopeful spirit held to the belief that there would be an explanation.

The nursery, the beautiful woman in the photograph, she could deal with those of course. It was just grist to the mill in these days of serial monogamy and transient relationships. The bag of money was more worrying, but wasn't it the reason she had approached him in the first place?

It was common knowledge he always had money in his pocket and paid for everything in cash. In this day of plastic payment it was odd and, coupled with his rough appearance and solitary nature, it singled him out. That's how the rumours began. The girl in the supermarket mentioned it to her boyfriend, the owner of the builder's yard told his buddies while they drank tea together and watched him choose his wire and fence posts, and so it grew.

None of it seemed important now, more than anything else she simply wanted his arms around her, his body warm against her skin and the comfort of his physical presence. She paced the floor, tried to peer out into the dark garden from her post in the centre of the room. He had told her to keep away from the windows and switching on the lights was out of the question. The shadows grew and the rain threw itself against the glass. Closing around her the night compounded her isolation. The world was filled with foreign noise, every slap and rattle made her jump. She wanted a drink but didn't want to make one, the noise of the kettle would be too loud and would mask the other noises that she didn't want to hear but couldn't bear to miss.

When the need to pee became undeniable she crept up the stairs. She was tentative and nervous and leaving the dark bathroom half fell back down the open staircase clinging to the banister to steady her panicked stumbling. If she had made a bid for freedom earlier in the day, which had been her first instinct, she would be in a place of light and movement by now, maybe on a warm bus with a cup of harsh coffee and the company of strangers. Tears filled her eyes; she hated to be afraid, she acknowledged how she had wound herself up into this panic but couldn't shake it; so she curled into a ball on the couch, coiled under the wool throw and gave herself up to misery and loneliness.

Despite the tension she did drift into a restless sleep, jerking awake with a painful suddenness in response to yet another clatter or creak. Eventually, her head fell back into the upholstered corner and her lips gaped a little as her breathing slowed and deepened, sleep held and soothed her for two short hours.

* * *

Her lids shot open, her heart was pounding and every nerve ending was tingling. It took a moment for her brain to catch up with her instincts but she was alive with tension. She dropped from the settee and scuttled on all fours into the corner. A faint click from the rear of the room caught her full attention now and she peered towards it. She could see nothing through the window save silver threads of rain lit by the moon. The bulk of the fell behind the house was a darker shadow against the night and the kitchen itself was a mass of shapes and silhouettes. Her ears stretched to listen and now picked up a gentle rattle. Wrapping her arms around her knees, squeezing into a tight ball she tried to melt into the darkness, her eyes darted back and forth, forced to look but afraid to see, afraid even to breathe.

The handle on the back door moved slowly downwards, smooth and quiet, the wood shifted inwards letting in the noise of the night and the chill and damp. A bulky shape formed, like a great dog, or a bear crawling forward on all fours.

"Sylvie."

The relief was dizzying.

"Sylvie, is that you?"

"Yes, what are you doing? What's wrong?"

"Quiet, keep quiet. Stay down. We need to get out. Can you crawl over here?"

In response she shuffled crabwise towards him.

"Samuel, what's going on?"

"Sshhh. We have to get away, I've been seen. I can't stay. The car is hidden, we need to grab what we can and go. I have to bring things from upstairs."

Chapter 24

"Stay here, don't stand up. I'm going upstairs to fetch our things."

He crawled away leaving Sylvie more panicked than before. His voice was tight with stress and urgency. Sliding across the floor he reached the bottom of the stairs and was now crouched low, running up the wooden steps.

Sylvie scanned the front windows but could see nothing, he had left the back door ajar and the sound of the teaming rain filled the room. Her hands shook and her stomach clenched with fear. She took a deep breath, it was time to throw aside this continual submission to the horror of what was happening and to take some control and at least think for herself.

Since Phil's murder she had been suspended, operating on a lower level than normal for her. Now, this surreal scene, Samuel disappearing in a frantic scuttle up the stairs, the dark house and the palpable air of danger jolted her into action.

She slithered across the smooth boards and followed him up to the landing. Together they dashed into the bedroom, he signalled for her to grab her bag. With a jolt of shock, she now remembered the tidying and sorting earlier in the day. She hissed at him.

"Samuel, I hung my clothes up."

He froze for a moment, then turned to her.

"Shit, why the hell…"

He shook his head then, reached across and squeezed her fingers.

"Can you reach them?"

"I'll try."

She rolled to the wall and pushed herself into a sitting position and then buttock-walked to the corner of the room, where the small closet was located. She reached up and grabbed the knob, swinging the door open only enough to allow her access. Now she rolled her whole body into the tiny built-in cupboard and in the darkness dragged the clothes downwards. The wooden hangers clattered and rattled causing a hiss of alarm from Samuel who was dragging his own luggage towards the bedroom door. As carefully as she could now she slid the remaining jeans and tops from the hangers dropping them to the floor. She crawled back across the bedroom, the pile of clothes bundled in front of her. She snatched her bag and dragged it nearer. In great handfuls she pushed and poked at the stuff forcing the zipper to close on the turmoil.

Though this aspect of the house could only be seen from the fell, he dragged her low beside him. They made their way back along the landing pushing and pulling at the bags. Samuel, crouching over bent knees struggled down the stairs juggling with the bulky holdalls. Sylvie followed, sitting on the steps and, childlike, sliding on her backside from one to the next until, nearly at the bottom, she launched herself forward then dropped to her knees to crawl across the floor.

"We can't clear up the kitchen, there's no way we can get the other stuff, we'll have to leave it. There's no time and I don't want us standing up, above the level of the windows. Bugger, bugger." He snorted with anger and frustration. "Sod it, we can't carry the stuff anyway."

"Is this my fault, Samuel, have I done this?"

"No, no. I've been followed, I was seen, or they traced my phone, God knows how. I think I gave them the slip but they could well be out there now, we can't risk it. It's not you though, they're not after you."

"Is it the police?"

"No, God, I wish it was, that'd be easy. I'll explain later. Look it's happened, there's no point moaning and the main thing now is to get away. Keep low and go out of the back door, stick by the house wall and turn left through the gate and right up the path onto the fell. The car is up there, it's not far but it's wet and muddy, don't slip. Go, go now. Quick as you can and don't wait, the key is in the car if I get stopped keep going and get away, as far as you can, as quick as you can, don't look back and don't wait. Now go!"

Her heart pounded, the muscles in her throat were tight with terror. Twice she lost her footing on the path which was slick with running mud. She reached out with her free hand tearing the skin on sharp gravel. The bag was unbelievably heavy and clumsy and the backpack, slung on one shoulder, slid forward banging against her side and the top of her thigh. Limping and lurching she kept on, desperate to look back but afraid of what she might see; she had to simply believe he was still there, tight behind her. Legs screaming with effort, gasping for breath she was aware only of the battle against the night, the slope of the hill and the gushing rain.

At last she had reached the beginning of the fell, the path flattened slightly before the steep climb; was this where he'd left the car? He hadn't told her. Which way should she go now in the rain-swept darkness? Desperately she spun on the soaking grass, her head flicking back and forth, she couldn't see more than a few yards ahead. Should she carry on upward or turn and run along the more level ground in the hope that she would see the bulk of the Land Rover? Surely, he couldn't have taken the car up onto the fell, but was it left or right now?

As she spun, peering into the darkness she felt the arms around her, she jerked spasmodically pushing backwards, squirming, raising her free hand to strike.

"It's okay, it's okay it's me."

He grabbed her arm and dragged her with him, struggling with two great bags in one hand, the weight dragging him sideways, his feet slipped and skidded on the uneven surface. Sylvie reached out to steady him and like a great crippled beast they pushed and pulled at each other staggering and lurching round the edge of the hill to where the car sat on a piece of flat ground, tight in against the slope. He dragged open the door, flung his things in and then turned to snatch her bags. He clambered up and across to the driver's seat. Before she had even closed the door the engine roared into life and using sidelights alone he moved across the broken, muddied surface, faster and faster over the grass and rock. She prayed he knew where he was going, that they wouldn't plummet into a gulley or career down the sheer side of the fell. She gripped the hand holds and jolting against the seat belts she clung on, gritted her teeth and prayed.

Chapter 25

The Land Rover slipped and slithered over the humps and rocks, even the four-wheel drive wasn't enough on this surface to make the ride secure. Sylvie clung to the strap above the door with one hand while the other braced against the dash board. The headlights flared on wet grass one moment, the tunnel of brightness startling against the dark, and then as the car was launched from a bump or boulder the beams would swing upward illuminating nothing but a sparkling curtain of slanting rain.

Samuel was tight with tension beside her, his hands locked around the wheel, the muscles of his neck and jaw knotted with stress and his eyes peering through the streaming windscreen.

* * *

When the willow fell it swept to the surface of the engorged torrent in a graceful swoon. The roots wrenched from the ground flinging mud, pebbles, small boulders and the moss and grass of the bank skywards. The whipping branches flew across the water to be grabbed and hurled downstream till their anchorage on the great trunk stayed them.

The river gushed into the hollow, washing away loose earth and debris and engulfing the tarpaulin and the body within. The recently loosened soil of the deep pit Samuel had dug swept away into the stream and the package moved and shifted, floating now, knocking against the sides of the grave. This rain had been the heaviest for more than a century, ground water from the hills and uplands gushed towards the coast raising the levels to beyond any in living memory. Eventually the ghastly parcel floated free of its berth, turned into the surge and bobbing and weaving on the currents it headed seaward with the rest of the debris.

* * *

The car raced over the grass and gravel until they connected with a narrow dirt road; with his intimate knowledge of the area Samuel was able to drive on sidelights, hurtling through the storm. He glanced into the rear-view mirror repeatedly and Sylvie swung round in the seat whenever the lurching ride allowed but neither saw any sign of a following vehicle.

After ten minutes they had reached a smooth metalled road, it was narrow and slippery in the wet but the driving was easier and the fear inside the little cab eased. Sylvie's hands dropped to her lap and she leaned back against the seat. Samuel rotated his neck and shoulders easing his muscles and they glanced at each other and grinned, it was close to hysteria but it felt like a victory.

"We need to get away and I think the best thing would be to go somewhere with plenty of people. I'm heading for Liverpool. It's about two hours, we'll use the motorway. The main thing now is to stay in the open."

"But what about the police, I thought we were trying to keep away from public places?"

"The game has changed, Sylvie. The police have probably no reason to even be looking for us yet. I had hoped we could get out of the country before Phil was missed but this is a different thing. This is me and what's happened to me."

He turned to look at her; his face was drawn and though the tension had eased, his eyes were tortured. She clenched her fists; she would ease this for him, open things up and straighten the tortured pathway.

"While you were out, I looked around the house, Samuel. I didn't mean to pry but I was bored. Anyway, whatever, I found the room, the nursery and a picture."

"I found a picture, you and a woman, a lovely woman. Pregnant I think."

"Marie."

The name crept from his lips, like a prayer or an invocation, barely heard above the rumble of the engine and the shush of the tyres on the wet surface. Sylvie reached across and touched his leg. He nodded briefly, just one small incline of his head. It was time to examine the truth.

Chapter 26

Bobbing and rolling, the sodden tarpaulin bundle sailed through the night. The cord Samuel had used to secure the ends began to unravel and the plastic sheet flapped against the wavelets.

It was noticed on the journey three times even though the night was black and it rained on, easier now but still torrential.

A farmer driving his beasts from the inundated fields flashed a torch beam over the banks and the running water. He was seeking stranded cattle and the passing shadow hardly registered, it wasn't his concern, his threatened herd filled his mind.

A policeman standing watch on an ancient bridge noted the thing as it snagged on the substructure drawing his gaze. At another time he would have climbed down, poked and pulled at the strange flotsam but tonight the passing vehicles, driving too fast for the conditions, flinging spray into the air and hurling yet more water at the buildings at risk of flooding were his concern, so he turned away consigning the thing to the storm and the night.

An old tramp down on the harbour side saw it drift through, by now the tarpaulin was mostly unwound. Phil's left arm had emerged to flop and slap, a useless stroke taking him nowhere. One leg gleamed intermittently when the roll turned him in the black water, pitching in the increased flow as the muddied, rubbish-strewn river met with the waves, crashing and beating against the sea wall. His brain tried to make sense of the messages his eyes sent but too many years at the end of a bottle and the need to find shelter overwhelmed any interest in the mystery and he turned away and scurried along the flooding streets.

Phil sailed onwards, his corpse bloated with gases of putrefaction, out along the seafront, pushed by the dying force of the river into the crashing waves. He washed back and forth for a while, hurled against the harbour wall, free now totally of the covering, arms and legs flailing, his head lolling loosely on the ruined neck and so out with the tide, out through the Bristol Channel and further into St George's Channel until, days later, decayed, pecked by sea birds and nudged and nibbled by fish, the remains sank to the peace of a watery grave joining the thousands of others, heroes and villains, who slumber forever in the depths.

He was missed briefly by his friends and even more fleetingly by the girls he had run. Benny found the car parked in the street outside his mother's house, the key hidden under the carpet. He took it for safekeeping; it was, after all, in better condition than his own. They asked around in the clubs and bars but no-one had seen him. They called on his mum but she had nothing she could tell them, his room was undisturbed, his phone was missing, she didn't know if he was coming back.

Occupied as she was with a new boyfriend and speculation that the shop where she worked was at risk of closure she had no room for concern regarding the eldest of her six children. He had gone bad and she felt his continued presence in her house to be an imposition and a risk. He was always at the edge of the law and she didn't need the police calling or his unpleasant, untrustworthy friends visiting. She told them he had gone, she didn't know where and didn't care.

There followed a few weeks of rumours: he had entered the witness protection programme or had moved to the north with Sylvie who was also missing. There was a report saying he had gone to London to join a gang there; had been seen running with a mob.

In truth no-one missed him, no-one wanted to speak to the police. So, Benny and Jake shared his stash of drugs, divided up the girls, and their dark and dirty world washed its hands of yet another piece of filth.

Ironically the storm had taken away the need to run but, long before Phil settled to the sea bottom, Samuel and Sylvie's lives had taken unforeseen roads and unlikely directions.

Chapter 27

Samuel swung into the car park at the motorway services; he lowered his forehead to rest on his hands where they lay on the steering wheel and let out a huge sigh before turning to her.

"Let's get some coffee."

They climbed down and hurried into the glaring brightness of the cafés and outlet shops, Samuel hauling the heavy holdall in his left hand.

The shock of normality, after the desperation and darkness of just a short while ago, left them disoriented and they reached for each other, walking through the bright spaces hand in hand.

In the toilets Sylvie stared at her reflection under the unforgiving lights. She looked the same as always, slightly bedraggled from the wind and rain of the car park and she acknowledged the dark smudges under her eyes, but really she appeared unchanged. How could this be? Her life had often been a struggle and it was easy to remember times of turmoil, when her dad was in jail and her mother drinking but this – murder, flight and real panic – it seemed impossible these things weren't drawn on her face.

She laid her hands flat on the Formica counter and braced her arms. Closing her eyes, she took in some deep breaths.

"Are you alright, love?" The gentle hand on her shoulder drew a squeal and jerk of shock.

"Oh sorry, sorry pet, I didn't mean to frighten you."

"No, no it's okay, I'm okay, thanks. Yes, I'm fine thanks."

The short dumpy woman smiled out from her simple, straightforward world as she reached over and patted at Sylvie's arm gently.

"You take care now, love. Bye bye."

"Yes, thanks. Bye."

Take care. She had tried, hadn't she? She had broken away from the destruction of her home life; true she had fallen in with Phil but she had tried to make something of her life, but maybe for some people there was no way to take care. In spite of every effort her life was to be cruel and harsh. She was swept with sadness, all she had ever wanted was peace and if possible a little happiness, was it too much to hope for? Eyes smarting with unshed tears, shoulders slumped, she drew away from the mirror and made her way back out to the hubbub and Samuel.

He was waiting by a clothes shop, flicking through the fleece tops, idling. She saw how he had positioned himself to keep a view of the main door reflected in the windows and although his hands rattled the hangers, sliding tops along the rail, his eyes were roaming back and forth around the whole space and then flicking to the window, monitoring continually. She watched him, how had she become involved with all of this and how had she let herself care? Her heart went out to him, sensing Samuel too needed peace and that his soul was tired.

She coughed before reaching out, he was wound tight and she didn't want to startle him, but he'd already seen her and smiled down as he turned and took her hand.

"Come on, Sylvie, time for coffee and conversation I think."

The tall cardboard beakers steamed gently on the table and they had both wrapped their fingers around the heat. Neither had raised the cups to drink. She looked into his face, tried to read the expression but the eyes were blank, closed off. It was as if he had gone inside himself searching for the way to begin. She wanted to help him.

"Was she your wife? Marie."

He shook his head, sharp and dismissive.

"We were going to get married, after the baby. She wanted a nice wedding, a big dress, flowers, so we were waiting. She was my life. All I ever needed was wrapped up in her."

"You were in the army, are you still? Is that what this is about, have you run away?"

He laughed but reached for her hand, wanting to let her know he wasn't laughing at her.

"No, I came out, they let me go. I joined the army from school pretty much, it was all I wanted to do and I loved it. Then I met Marie and I didn't love it quite so much because it took me away from her. She was patient and kind and said she was happy for me to stay and have my career and we'd find a way to make it work. We did, for a while we did," he explained.

"I grew up in the house, where we just were. It was Mum and Dad's place, they had it from new and then when they died I took it over. He worked for the National Park and Mum was a receptionist at the doctors, but they died within a couple of years of each other. It was okay really, sad, you know, for me, but they were old when I was born and they'd had good lives. I kept the house on because it had always been a happy place and it was somewhere solid and secure. Marie was a teacher and she got work in the school, just part time but she did other stuff, exam marking, a bit of extra tuition; it all worked well and she loved it there as much as I always had," he continued.

"Anyway, I was posted to Afghanistan. The first tour was hard on us but we got through it and then the baby happened, not really planned but we loved the idea."

By now his eyes had filled with tears which he needed to brush from his cheeks with the back of a hand. The other hand was gripping Sylvie's as if it was a life line, the only thing that saved him from being swept away by the grief, which she saw in every line of his face.

"People here wonder why we're fighting there, well I wondered as well. Most of the time you're with people who either don't want us there or just want whatever they can get from us. They neither know nor care whether we're American or British or any of the others, they just want dollars and favours or they want us gone.

You can't tell who is the enemy, you talk to an old man and his son one day and they smile at you and then the next day the son is shooting at you from behind some crappy half-built house. It's hard and uncomfortable and soul destroying. Blokes commit suicide, lose limbs, are blown to smithereens, go mental. So, you ask why are we here and they tell you it's to keep the UK safe. To stop the drugs trade and to fight terrorism. You make yourself believe it because if you don't then all the lads who have died and all the endless hours sitting on some bloody sand dune staring into nothing – too hot in the summer, too cold in the winter – all of it is for nothing unless you believe."

He paused, stared around the place as though surprised to find himself there, in a service station in the rain. His eyes swung downwards, to glare into the coffee.

"So, Marie went with her mum to London, to buy some stuff for the baby, just a day out for fun."

He stopped speaking and blinked rapidly, swallowed hard and then tried a couple of times to carry on, his throat working, tension evident in every inch of his body. He coughed.

"She was hit by a car, they both were. They were killed outright. Three generations wiped off the face of the earth in an instant."

Sylvie was crying openly now, her hand covered her mouth but her eyes never left his face.

"The car was driven by a drug dealer being chased by the police, and it didn't stop. The police had to because of Marie and her mum and my baby, my poor little baby who didn't even have the chance to be born, and the scum got away.

So, there I was stuck in the arsehole of the world fighting to make the UK safe and the only thing I cared about, the only two things I had to love were wiped out by some scumbag dealing drugs. Where's the sense in that, eh, where's the justice? How did I keep them safe?"

He looked at her now, deep into her eyes, though he must have known she had no answers for him, he had no answers for himself. He shook his head and grabbed the coffee cup and gulped the cooling drink. It was a subterfuge, just to give himself time to carry on. Now he had started, he was determined she would know it all.

Chapter 28

Sylvie could think of nothing to say to him, this raw pain was too much to deal with, so she simply stroked the back of his hand and waited until he was ready.

"The army let me go, on compassionate grounds. I was no good to them, no good to anyone for a long time; so I drifted. I couldn't go back to the house, I didn't have any other place, so I dossed with some mates here and there, slept at homeless shelters, whatever suited me at the time.

"Slowly I came back, from the worst of it, but the world didn't make sense any more. I didn't know what to do, how to get back on track. Anyway, then one day, down in London, I saw a young lad being beaten up. It was one of those things, three on one, he was on the floor and I just jumped in. I know I was out of control, I was vicious, brutal. I suppose there was some pent-up fury, whatever. I just remember it felt good to be hurting someone, I know that's awful but right then it felt better than anything had for months."

He reached across now with his other hand and took her slim one in both of his.

"I was out of control, totally. In the end they ran off and I helped the kid up. Turns out he was a runner for a drug gang and the scum I had just beaten up were from another crew; oh shit, it was just the same garbage that goes on all over the place. It sickened me, this was the world that had killed Marie and the baby and Marie's mum. It was rotten, stinking and then I saw what I could do. The army had taught me a lot of things, most of all they had taught me how to fight."

He paused, raised his head and looked into her eyes. Do you want to know this stuff, Sylvie? It's not nice, are you okay with this?"

She nodded and managed to smile at him.

"Okay, well I went on a bit of a vigilante spree. I roamed the streets, I hurt some people. Some of them were injured really badly, I don't know if they all recovered. I didn't care much. I slept at hostels and in squats, I was invisible and at night I went out and hurt people. It was animal, inhuman, I thought I was doing a good thing, revenge, getting even and so on, but really I think I was just living on hate and it was eating me up," he said.

"After a while a mob down there approached me, they knew what I'd been doing; they wanted me to work with them. Can you imagine? After what had happened they actually thought I could become one of them," he continued.

"I played along, made the right noises, flattered them, used the skills I had learned courtesy of Her Majesty's armed forces. I got in with the movers and shakers, right up to the top. They were stupid, really just thuggish idiots but I played their game."

"Sylvie, I know you looked in the bag," Samuel said, and raised his hand as she opened her mouth to speak, staying the lie that had leapt to her lips.

"It's okay, really. It's what I would have done. I do understand. It's dirty money, Sylvie, it's taken from the people who tried to recruit me. I left them all in a burning building, I don't know how many survived, I honestly don't care. But they do they care very much and since then I have been moving, running. I thought, in the woods, the shack, I was safe for a while but it couldn't last. They'll get me in the end I know, I've accepted it, but not you, this isn't your world, not your problem, you have to get away. They've found me again, I managed to get away yesterday. Somebody must have seen us at the house, whatever, it doesn't really matter. I know it's only a question of time, they won't give up. Each time I escape it's just avoiding the inevitable."

"I'm tired of it; to be honest I'm not sure I really have the heart to run anymore. Part of me just wants it to be over, I won't give up without a fight but really I just want it done. But you, you have to be safe, Sylvie, I don't want what I've done to hurt you."

"Samuel, go to the police. Can't you tell them, give them the money, they have protection things don't they, you could have a new identity, go abroad, anything."

"Oh, Sylvie, you don't know though, you have no idea the things I've done, the people I've hurt, probably killed. No, it's all gone too far."

She saw him switch off. He was drained by the confession, by reliving the horrors and the guilt. They sat hand in hand for long minutes as the world swirled around them, together in their loneliness, knowing they were probably lost to each other already.

She whispered now, as her hand curled in his and the tears began to dry on her cheeks.

"What should we do now then, where will we go, Samuel? Can I stay with you, for a while at least? I'm not scared you know, I can help you, maybe we can get away, go to America. You have all the money. Don't give up. Samuel, I think I love you. I know you can't feel the same, you have Marie and the baby in your heart and there's no room left for me and I don't expect you to, but can we be together, just for a while?"

When he raised his face there was such sadness there that she couldn't bear to look at him. She turned away.

"Samuel, there are some men by the car. Oh God, is it them? Shit."

He leapt up dragging her with him.

Chapter 29

Samuel dragged her towards the front door, she pulled back, afraid of the car park. His grip on her wrist was painful and she was aware of people staring as they shuffled past.

"Samuel wait, they're out there, they'll see us. Wait, come the other way."

"No, there's no way out, those doors are locked and alarmed, trust me, just come on now, quick."

They slid through the great doors and turned sharply left, away from the car and towards the coach and lorry parking area.

It was still raining, everything was sodden; they ran through the puddles, muddy, oily water splashing up around their feet, soaking their shoes and clothes. He wove between the great trailers dragging her behind him and hefting the heavy bag. A driver climbing down from his cab collided with Samuel.

"Hey, you stupid bugger, watch where you're going, asshole."

"Sorry, we're sorry."

Sylvie gasped an apology and twisted to smile at the man but he'd turned his back and lowered his head as he stomped towards the lights of the building. There were a number of trucks parked up. Many of them had the curtains pulled over the windscreens, the drivers sleeping away the hours until they could legally get back behind the wheel. He ignored those and the ones that were obviously local, based in Preston, Lancaster, Morecombe, there was no point stowing away on something only going five miles down the road, or worse still which had only just left the depot and wouldn't be stopping again until Portsmouth or Dover.

A great red truck with a curtain sided trailer attracted Samuel, he laid his hand on the bonnet. Cold, the cab empty but not curtained, the depot in Liverpool. They were on the southbound carriageway and so by deduction it was a safe bet this guy had been heading for home. Probably his tachograph had demanded he stop, so he had slept away the day and had now gone in to the toilet or for a cup of coffee and some carbs before finishing his delayed journey. He would be annoyed because he hadn't made it home in time and hopefully he was less likely to do much checking before he got back on the road, especially in the rain and cold.

Putting his finger to his lips to warn Sylvie against speaking, he took a knife from his pocket. He cut an L-shaped slit in the heavy siding, he lifted the edge to peer inside. The truck was part loaded with wooden boxes, tied and secured, and he judged it to be as safe as they could hope for.

He ran around the back without much hope and, as expected, the doors were padlocked. Using two hands he stretched the gap he had made in the curtain.

"Do you think you can get in here, if I lift you up?"

She nodded and raised her hands to hoist herself towards the entrance he'd made, holding the wet curtain away from her face. Wrapping his arms around her, he lifted her to the space and she slithered inside on her belly, kicking and squirming. It was dark, dirty and unpleasant and she was terrified. As soon as her legs were in, she rolled over onto her behind and pushed herself into a sitting position. Shakily she rose to her feet, Samuel was pushing the bag of money in through the hole and she bent down to grab it with both hands and drag it across the scarred wooden boards. He followed and then turned to pull the trailer side back into place. He couldn't do much, but it was taut and would face away from the wind as the truck moved. Providing the driver didn't examine his charge on this cold, wet night they should get away with it – all they could do was hope.

The light was very dim, only the glow from a small window in the roof, but Samuel checked the strapping on the boxes; watching him Sylvie saw this wasn't the first time he had done this. He shoved and pushed at the load testing it for movement, though it had obviously been okay for the first part of its journey. He turned back to her and tried a smile, it was a valiant effort under the circumstances but it was empty; she took what she could from it and curved her lips upwards in response.

There was a pile of dirty blankets neatly folded in the corner near to the back doors and Samuel pointed to them, she nodded and flopped down onto the hard, makeshift seat. Her insides were in turmoil, this was very frightening. She had no idea what it would be like when this great leviathan moved off but she didn't expect it to be pleasant; she was cold, wet and scared. Samuel lowered himself to the floor, wrapped his big arms around her and hugged her to him. She laid her head on his shoulder and relinquished all responsibility for what was happening, her eyelids closed squeezing out two fat tears which dribbled down her cheeks and, unregarded, dripped away to be lost in the muck and moisture on her jeans.

She had never felt so tired, so dreadfully weary or so utterly content all at the same time. She was shivering, from fear and cold, but as his body heat and the strength of him leached into her bones, she relaxed and let herself drift in the dark, cold void that held her now.

Chapter 30

The movement in the back of the trailer wasn't as bad as Sylvie had feared. It was disconcerting to hear the traffic swooshing by on the road without a view of it, but the rocking was soothing and they sat cradled together, silent in their exhaustion.

She had left everything behind save the things in her handbag, her phone was there but the battery had died long since and with no charger it was useless. Samuel had flung his from the car window before they had reached the service station. She had some money, not much, her debit and credit cards and some bits and pieces of cosmetics. Samuel must have even less, only what he had in his pockets and anything else stuffed in the big bag along with the money.

It was liberating, she felt cut loose, free-floating. Nothing to hold her to her past life and no evidence of where she came from. She relished her new-found anonymity until, mulling it over in her mind, she realised she had no means of identification. Her driving licence was back in her other bag; at first she didn't mind, thought it didn't matter. She could change her name, re-invent herself, her past was in the car park on the motorway.

With this thought the fragile sense of peace deserted her, bursting like a soap bubble in the rain and she shot upright. Samuel had been snoozing but now he was alert and awake, his head flicked back and forth.

"What, what is it?"

"My driving licence, it's in my bag, in the car. They've got my name, my old address, the flat. There're some photographs in there as well, me and Phil."

He didn't speak but merely drew her closer to him, they both knew she was now complicit, her name was linked indelibly with his. No matter what, she was a part of his problems and had taken on board all the things he was fighting with and fleeing from. They didn't know Phil was no longer a threat; the great storm had taken him from their lives forever.

For a moment she buried her head in his chest. What did it mean? She raised her eyes to his.

"Shit, Samuel, I guess we're stuck with each other now."

Surprisingly he grinned at her, bent and kissed her forehead.

"Well, I think you may be right."

There was nothing they could do and so, accepting the reality, they settled in the cold darkness of the trailer and listened to each other breathing.

* * *

In little over an hour the speed changed and there was a difference in noise. They had left the motorway and were weaving through urban streets. Samuel moved across the wooden boards and lay down in front of the slit in the vinyl; he lifted it and peered into the night.

"Looks like we're nearly there, wherever 'there' might be. Can you push the bag over? Be careful stay on your bottom, don't stand in case he goes round a corner. Slide across. Be ready to jump out if he stops."

They waited tense and watchful; Samuel held the gap open, waiting for the truck to pull over.

"When I tell you to go, just jump out and get to safety as quick as you can. Then, no matter what, stay where you are. I will try to get out at the same time but if I can't I'll come for you. I promise you, okay?"

She nodded and reached up to kiss him briefly on the mouth.

"What I said, in the café, about the way I feel."

He nodded.

"I meant it. I really do care about you, Samuel. No matter what happens I want you to know I really do care."

"I know."

He didn't say anymore but turned back to the slit, peering out into the rain-swept night.

"Right, now, jump down."

The truck was stopped at a six-road junction, the lights were red, there was little traffic. He held the space open as Sylvie lowered herself backwards dropping the last few feet and then he threw the bag after her. He turned and came behind her lowering himself almost to the road and then letting go with his hands, landing with his knees bent. He grabbed the bag and pushed Sylvie ahead of himself onto the pavement and into the darkness of a shop doorway as the truck drew away, onwards towards the city.

"Are you okay, not hurt?"

"No, no I'm fine, are you?"

"Yeah, no problem. Okay, first of all, let's see if we can work out where we are. Come on, which way, left or right, it doesn't matter, you choose."

"Oh, erm, okay left, let's go left."

It was cold, wet and inhospitable. They were on the outskirts of a city, they assumed it to be Liverpool but as yet had no real proof. It was a main road of shops and garages. There was a glow in the sky, the promise of bigger things a few miles distant. Here there were a couple of small supermarkets still open and the ubiquitous kebab shops and pizza places. The electric colours spilled out to shimmer in kaleidoscopes on flagstones soaked by the continual downpour. Wet litter shifted in the cold wind and they had to jump back from the kerb as cars sped past sending great fountains across the pavement.

Samuel stopped outside a snack bar.

"Are you hungry?"

"No, I'm not hungry, I could use a drink, just some water or juice but I don't want to eat anything."

"Hang on then."

He went into a small convenience store, came out with cartons of juice and a bottle of water. He had bought some chocolate and broke a piece from the bar and fed it to her.

"You have to keep your sugar levels up. It's cold and we might have to walk for a bit."

As he spoke they saw, up ahead, a bus stop with a small queue of people huddling under the meagre shelter. Samuel spoke to a couple standing with arms wrapped around each other, locked together, looking spaced out.

"Excuse me mate, can we get a bus here for the town centre do you know?"

"Yeah, number thirty-six takes you in. Where're you going?"

"We just need to get into town, find somewhere to stay. We were supposed to be going away." He hefted the bag as evidence of the trip, "But we had some trouble, my mate was taken ill now we just need a place for tonight."

"Well if you get the number thirty-six it'll take you in, but you could stay at the place up the road if you only need somewhere to sleep." He pointed towards a building, a large house, a few hundred yards away from where they stood. There was an illuminated sign on a post in the almost empty front garden which had been tarmacked over to form a car park.

"Oh, right. We didn't see that, do you know if it's okay?"

"Yeah, my mate's mum runs it. It's not dear and you get a brilliant fry up for breakfast. Tell 'em Stano sent you."

Samuel stretched out his hand and the youth simply knocked at it with the back of his knuckles.

"Thanks, Stano."

"No problem."

He turned his attention back to the spliff his girlfriend had been holding out to him.

The hotel was small, old-fashioned and warm. It smelled of dust and cooking but it was clean. The middle-aged woman who opened the door had a friendly smile, a spare room and a nod when they mentioned Stano.

"Mates rates then for you."

She grinned as she said it and they all acknowledged the emptiness of the statement. She pushed the register across the top of a small wooden counter positioned in the corner of the hallway.

Without a moment of hesitation Samuel signed them in as Mr and Mrs S Percy.

"Have you some ID?"

"We lost some of our bags, is it going to be a problem?" Sylvie stood silent at his side, afraid to speak in case she spoilt the confident act.

"Well, normally I've to keep to the rules, but seeing as you know Stano." Again she grinned. "Are you paying with a card? Cos if you are, I need to take it now."

"Cash okay?"

She nodded.

"Just one night?"

"I think so, if it changes is that okay?"

"'Course, let me know before twelve that's all. Double room, fifty for cash."

She grinned at him as the tax man was denied his cut. Samuel winked at her, unzipped the bag top and bending low to block her view he slid out some notes handing them over in a crumpled bunch. She stroked at them, easing out the creases, a questioning look on her face.

"It's not hot this, is it?"

"No, we haven't got cards, we had to go bankrupt, bloody bankers."

The story was familiar and she accepted it with a nod.

"Bloody bankers, sodding government, sod the lot of 'em I say. Well, you guys have a good sleep, breakfast from seven-thirty to nine-thirty and you have the room till twelve, less you tell me otherwise. Okay?"

"Thanks."

The key was attached to a large wooden fob painted with a number eight.

"Second floor, have you just the one bag?"

"Yes, thanks, it's fine we can manage. Can we get a cup of tea?"

"Kettle and stuff in the room love. Do you want a sandwich or something?"

Samuel glanced at Sylvie, she simply shook her head. Her mind was already full with thoughts of a hot shower, clean sheets and stretching out beside Samuel. It felt like years since they lay together in the little room in the Lake District.

Chapter 31

The walls ran with steam, hot water beat down on Sylvie's head – it was bliss. Their filthy clothes were draped around the room dripping onto the grey and pink floral carpet. She had washed her underwear in the tiny sink and put it to dry on the radiator. It was the best they could manage, but feeling warm, safe and clean was enough, for now.

The cubicle door slid back.

"Sylvie?"

She nodded and his bulky body filled the moist space. Wrapped in the circle of his arms she felt his skin begin to warm and the tension leave his muscles. His hands were in her hair now, fingers raking it back pulling the tendrils away from the wet of her face. She stared into his eyes till he bent to her, his lips brushed her neck. Thrills of passion skittered through her body taking the strength from her legs.

Clinging together they revelled in the comfort of heat and cleanliness until the closeness of their bodies, the touch of skin on skin and the evidence of his growing passion forced them back into the bedroom. Afterwards, sleepy and fulfilled they dragged the covers back and coiled together, put aside the mounting problems and future dangers and surrendered to exhaustion…

A door slamming further along the hallway brought Samuel to his senses. For a minute he lay still, his arm had curled in sleep to cuddle the slight body beside him. Her hair spread across the pillows and her face, in repose, looked heartbreakingly childlike.

He was troubled; this girl had turned his life on its head. Everything he thought he had forfeited, the feelings he had subdued, interaction with other people – pleasure, passion and hope – she was relighting them all. The flame of life had been rekindled and he didn't know how he felt about it.

She was so very different from what he had first expected. Though life had hardened her, she was in truth soft and gentle, caring and vulnerable. He wanted her to be safe, wanted to spend some time with her. He had chosen to live an empty, lonely life, punishing himself for continuing to survive when Marie and the baby were dead. He had felt his existence to be a burden and many times he'd considered leaving it all behind, taking what he thought of as the easy way out. Now though, with Sylvie he had someone else to consider, he couldn't leave her on her own to face the danger she had inadvertently walked into.

Tenderly he brushed the hair from her face and kissed her awake; she stretched, cat-like and slid her arms around his neck kissing him back, warm and sleepy, still part lost in her dreams. It reminded him painfully just what it was like to wake with someone who cares. Was he ready to experience all this again, and in truth could he even begin to hope for it with all the ugliness and pain in the past and the undeniable danger in the future? It was too late to think 'if only' and he wasn't sure there was any room for 'what if'.

Chapter 32

After breakfast they pushed their overloaded bellies back up the narrow stairs and walked hand in hand to their room. Though they had brushed and cleaned their clothes with the small means available they knew they looked scruffy and unkempt, even in these modest surroundings. Samuel walked to the window, lifted the floral net and peered out, left and right.

"I think we could stay here another night. We need to sort out some clothes and bags and stuff, what do you think? We could go to the shops and buy what we need. I could tell reception we'll stay on."

"Yes please, it'd be nice to have a place to come back to. Samuel, are we okay here? They can't find us can they, I mean they've no idea where we are, they can't know, so we're safe aren't we?"

"I wish I could tell you yes, but I have to say that in all honesty I just don't know. I've been places where I would have never believed I could be recognised, where I've never set foot before and then after a couple of days I've had to leave again. They are amazing, their web stretches over the whole country. They're interlinked, many parts of the same families, cousins, brothers and they have a wonderful communication network, they all seem to know almost by instinct when one is in danger or when someone has crossed them. These aren't little dragged-together dealers, this is a huge organisation. All I can say is that for today I think we should be okay, but they're very likely to work out how we came here, to Liverpool anyway. They know we didn't have the car, they know there was probably nothing other than the trucks, and they'll piece it together," Samuel replied

"I threw my laptop into the lake when I first saw they were following me but I don't know how much access they might have to my email. I don't think we can risk trying to get your passport now, I can't put my contact in danger, I won't do that. We'll have to come up with something else," he continued.

He put his arms around her, she was so small and frightened and he felt a deep need to protect her. He hadn't been there to save Marie but maybe he could find a way to save this girl. Perhaps that's what this was about – recompense and restitution. It was too late for him, he knew, but she hadn't done anything wrong and didn't deserve to be caught up in his mess.

"Come on, grab your coat, we'll go and get the bus, buy some stuff and have a drink. At the end of the day what's going to happen will happen and staying in here isn't an option."

"I haven't got much money. Will it be okay if I use my cards?"

"No, not now they have your name and address. Don't worry about it. It's time I spent some of the money, I've dragged it around with me long enough."

"Why can't you put it in the bank? You know, in bits, so it doesn't look odd?" Sylvie asked.

"I haven't got an address. You have to have an address to open an account. The house in the Lakes was in Marie's name, all the bills and so on; we thought it best, to make it easy if anything happened to me in Afghanistan. We never imagined it could be the other way round. I haven't lived there or paid the bills in my own name for years."

"But what about before, when you had just come out of the army and stuff? Didn't you have an account then?"

"Yes, of course but I spent it all, emptied the accounts. I didn't work and then I just lived on what I could scrounge. I was so lost, Sylvie, things like money, houses, they meant nothing to me. I was in a dark hole and the real world couldn't reach me. Anyway, the top and bottom of it is that the money for the bills at the house, the council tax and stuff, the cleaner, it all comes out of an account automatically, I had my army salary paid into it and I suppose now my pension. I guess it's all just ticking over. To be honest I don't know and I have never cared enough to check, it could be that the government are after me as well. Now it wouldn't be safe to start using it, the cards are out of date and I never collected the replacements, it's just too complicated. No, it's all cocked up to be honest. The cleaner is from before, she never asked any questions, the last time I saw her was after the funeral. She assumed I was going back to Afghanistan and I let her. People don't bother if their lives aren't touched. I suppose now though she's going to wonder, with all the things we had to leave. This gang have people everywhere. It's a massive organisation; they work in banks and government offices. They fund arms smuggling, people trafficking, paedophile rings, the drugs of course and terrorism. That's another reason they won't let up on me, I know too much," Samuel said.

"I didn't realise, I thought it was just a couple of pushers, like Phil and Benny."

"No, it's not, it's a different world."

He pursed his lips, shook his head. Lost in the morass as he had been, home had been unreachable, he had let it all go, part of a life he no longer had. It was impossible to even guess what the situation was, maybe he should try and find out. Could he do it without drawing attention to himself, and did he really want to? There was no going back, but when danger threatened he had run instinctively to the place of peace. He should probably leave it in the past, it had served a purpose and now it was dangerous there. He didn't know who had seen them, who was in the pay of the gang, but someone was; someone had watched and reported back – the thought was chilling. He had lived there all his life and even that was tainted now.

He put it from his mind, some things can't be fixed and he had a rare chance to take some pleasure from today. He would give Sylvie a bundle of cash and enjoy watching her spend it. It had never felt like stolen money. He had taken it from the scum he left to burn to death, payment for the things they had made him do and compensation for a future he had been denied.

He dragged the hold-all from under the bed and took out two handfuls of notes.

"Here, there looks to be plenty there, let's go and spend it."

She gasped as she took hold of the bundles.

"It's all fifties and twenties, I've never held so much money. They can't trace it can they?"

"I don't think so, it's what I've lived on for a few years now, to buy food and stuff and they never did find me in the woods so I guess it's okay. Anyway, what else can we do? You know, Sylvie, this is all going to end at some time, I'm in the open now, they know I'm still alive and they'll keep on looking until they find me. They have long memories and these people, they don't let things go. I can't make you any promises, all I can say is, any time you want to go, just go. I'll give you money, help you to get away."

The look on his face told her far more than the words he was saying. She knew if she was to leave him now it would be the end of him, either he would force things to a climax with the drug gang or he would simply go away and allow himself to die. Like a wounded beast he would give up the fight. She shook her head and stared deep into his eyes, she wouldn't verbalise her thoughts. If he didn't understand yet that she was committed, she didn't know how to tell him.

Chapter 33

They pushed the bag under the bed as far as they could reach, in terms of security it was a joke but there was no other option. Samuel knew he'd be better off without it. He had tried once to throw it away, even getting as far as the banks of a reservoir, but in the end the sheer amount of money held him back. It had cost so much in personal anguish and now it had become a liability in itself and he didn't know what to do. He had considered leaving it outside a charity shop but they would probably notify the police and it would possibly lead back to him. The army had his fingerprints after all. What had seemed a prize had become a burden and he kicked it under the bed and turned away, locking the room door and leaving the key at reception.

The rain had stopped at last, though it was dull and chilly. They walked to the bus stop and joined the queue; nobody looked at them except for one old woman dragging a tartan shopping trolley. She smiled and nodded before turning back to gaze up the road. Most people were texting or simply staring blankly into the distance. A double-decker rumbled to a stop and the line shuffled forward; no-one paid the driver, they simply flashed cards and passes in his direction and he nodded curtly.

"We need to get to the town centre, how much for two returns?"

"Where abouts ya going?"

"Somewhere near the shops."

"Lime Street, it'll be three pound ten pence. I'll give you a shout."

"Thanks mate."

"Yeah."

The bus drew away and they had to stagger to the nearest free seats, holding on to the hanging straps and bars. Sylvie had wanted to go upstairs, wanted to see Liverpool unfolding before her. She had never been so far away from home before and this city with its history and pop culture fame excited her.

"Do you know Liverpool, Samuel?"

"Not so much, I think it's changed a lot in the last few years. When I was a kid, a teenager, we used to come now and again, it was quite a stretch but sometimes a gang of us would do the trip. I should think I can find my way about, it's quite compact in the centre, all the shops and so on are pretty close. Near the station and St John's Market."

"Can we go and see The Cavern, you know, the Beatles place?"

"Well, you can but it's not in Matthew Street any more, it's been moved and I think that misses the point, doesn't it?"

Disappointment clouded her face and he realised she was treating the trip as a day out, a mini break. She truly had no idea the danger they were in. He didn't want the spark of excitement to fade from her eyes and so he pushed the worries away.

"You can see the ferries though, on the Mersey, and the Liver Birds and so on. I think I can get us to there from Lime Street. There are some beautiful buildings and there are some Beatles memorials and stuff," he said.

"Great, it's silly I suppose but I love the Beatles, my mum used to play them and it always seemed to me that it must have been a brilliant time, the sixties, all the stuff that went on."

"Yes, of course I missed it but my mum had friends who knew Liverpool well and they used to talk about it. I don't think they realised at the time what a difference it would make to the city. Up until then it was all faded glory with the docks in trouble from union disputes and the big boats, liners, not coming so much. It's a place that seems to go up and down, riding high for a few years and then down in the doldrums. Anyway we'll have a wander round." He took hold of her hand and tucked it into the fold of his arm.

The little glow of happiness had touched him, how much had he lost? So many precious days he had spent in the dark and now, with this little scrap of a girl the curtains were drawing back. He wasn't sure he could do it, it had been too long and he couldn't convince himself there could be a future, the trouble he was in was overwhelming. When he fired the warehouse with the gang members locked inside he had known he was throwing away his life and acknowledged that on some level it was deliberate. He didn't want it, the empty existence, without Marie he was on a suicide trip and he was just trying to take as many of them with him as he could.

Was it his time now, could he go back to hope and love and fun? He couldn't remember a time not drenched in misery. What if it was time to let himself begin to feel again, where could it go? They couldn't have a life together just running continually to stay alive. He heaved a great sigh, it was never going to be possible to start again, he had gone too far. So, today would be what it was and if there was a tomorrow he would take it as well but he wouldn't think ahead more than that.

After a drive of about thirty minutes the driver yelled out.

"Lime Street, here you are mate. I hope you've got ya money ready, she's got a glint in her eye, your bird."

They clambered down from the bus into the hurly burly of the city, she felt anticipation and excitement the like of which she hadn't experienced since she was a child.

In a very short time they had bought jeans and sweatshirts, socks, spare trainers, underwear and things for sleeping in. They had soap and shampoo, Sylvie had some creams and deodorants and he had insisted she buy herself a bracelet she'd tried on. He fastened it around her wrist and planted a kiss on her smiling mouth. They could have been any young couple, out on a spree that would leave them eating beans for the last days of the month or maxing out on cards which would wait in ambush for them on pay-day.

The bag of money, the spectre of history with Phil and other dreadful memories tucked away in the back of Samuel's mind were walled up, not allowed out, they were having fun and, as young animals will, they lost sight of the danger prowling on the dark edges of reality.

Chapter 34

An Italian restaurant in a refurbished fruit market restored their flagging energy with pasta and wine. Later, they looked at the river sliding past and the great white birds watching out from their shackled perches high above the Three Graces. They wandered the old streets and the new malls. Sylvie was entranced.

On the walk back to the bus station she cried out.

"Oh look, what's that? See there, the sculpture, do you know what it is, Samuel?"

He shook his head as they walked across the pavement to stand beside the bronze of a woman perched on a bench feeding birds. It was poignant and beautiful. Eleanor Rigby.

Sylvie swiped away a stray tear, both were lost in their own thoughts of what might have been, hopes of what could be and wishes too precious to be acknowledged.

"Poor little thing, she looks so lonely, so brave but, oh I don't know, empty. I know it's because of the song but doesn't she look lonely, Samuel?"

He nodded at her, then read the little plaque, "To all the lonely people". It touched him. It was him, wasn't it? Lonely, brutalised and unwanted, and Sylvie, though she had lived with people, they didn't value her, didn't care; so she was just as alone in her different way. Marie, in those last moments, dying on the street while he was thousands of miles away, even though she carried their child, had she been lonely and frightened. He couldn't bear it, couldn't let the thoughts creep in again, he had driven them away and no matter what, he must not go there again. All the lonely people.

He turned and strode off drawing her after him and in silence they made their way back to the bus stop and the number thirty-six.

The little hotel welcomed them, the windows blazed with orange light and the sign in the car park was a beacon in the gathering dusk, it was a happy thing that they had a place to come home to.

They collected the key and toted the bags upstairs, it was warm after the rawness of the wind and they were looking forward to the shower, a lie down and then they would venture out again in their new clothes, to find somewhere to eat.

As the door swung open, their fragile world spun and collapsed into a vortex of disbelief and fear.

"Ah, you're back, at last." The voice was calm, quiet and yet immensely threatening, the gun was terrifying and the atmosphere electric.

Samuel pushed Sylvie behind him, tried to shield her from the man sitting at ease on the bed. He was thrusting her away, trying to force her back into the hallway.

"Christ, Sylvie, run. Run!"

She was petrified by fear and indecision and the moment was lost. The hefty thug had left the bed, crossed the room and, pushing against the wood, installed himself between them and the only means of escape. The gun was levelled directly at Sylvie, she had instinctively reached out towards Samuel but her hand was grasped and twisted backwards so, with an ease born of long experience, he held her captive and in pain in front of him.

"Let her go. Just let her go. She has nothing to do with anything. Let her go."

"Oh, I don't think so." As he spoke the gunman twisted Sylvie's arm causing her to screech. "Quiet now, bitch, don't want you raising an alarm, quiet or I'll just off your boyfriend here and now, then we'll see what fun we can have you and me."

She gulped back the tears, her body shook, she stared at Samuel the terror in her eyes tearing at his heart. He hadn't had a chance to take it in yet, reality had turned on its head in an instant, leaving no time to react.

"Better still, why don't we just get it together now, I'm sure you'd enjoy a little pantomime wouldn't you, Samuel? How are you anyway? It seems like such a long time since we saw you. You've been missed, you have no idea how much we wanted to see you; to have some time with you. I wanted to show you this for one thing."

He held out his hand, the one holding the gun. The skin was puckered and red, the little finger missing and the ring finger twisted and deformed.

"Now how do you think that happened? Well, I burned it you see, on a red-hot door handle. Silly of me, wasn't it."

As he spoke, he swung his fist sideways. The flying blow connected with Samuel's face, the grip of the gun tore at his cheek and split his lip, blood flooded down his chin to drip onto the front of his jacket. He staggered backwards but didn't fall, Sylvie squealed again.

"Oh see, I just can't control it, all spoiled and bent as it is."

He powered the deformed hand back the other way, Samuel's jaw cracked upwards and he yelled out as a splinter of tooth flew across the space between him and Sylvie. Her knees buckled as her world spun and reddened, the brute holding her had to bend and wrap his arm around her waist to hold her upright.

"Now then, boys and girls, here's what we're going to do. You…" He pointed at Samuel who was leaning back against the bed holding his bleeding mouth. "…Are going to sit down and be very, very quiet."

He bent over so his cheek was touching Sylvie's, she tried to pull away but he simply tightened his grip around her stomach, she gasped. "You are going to be a very good girl, a very good little girl."

He dragged her towards the small chair in the corner and pushed her roughly into it. Moving round to stand directly in front of her he bent low. She could smell garlic and tobacco on his breath, his eyes were cold, brown stones lit by tiny starbursts where the light from the hotel sign in the garden glinted on the irises.

Samuel had straightened. Possibly he had hoped to make use of the moment to launch an attack, possibly he was dizzied and disoriented by the blows to his face. No matter, he moved. The gunman swung in an instant and the world exploded in noise and a flash. Sylvie screamed as, for a moment, the universe froze.

Chapter 35

As her hearing returned, Sylvie's head filled with the sound of slamming doors, shouts and thundering footsteps. Despite his earlier cool, the gunman was now obviously panicked. It was clear he had acted spontaneously and this wasn't the way he had intended the scene to play out.

He strode to the door and yanked it open. Already the uproar had begun to subside. It had been one loud bang then nothing and in the absence of alarms and sirens most people seemed to be accepting nothing too awful had happened.

He pushed the door closed, turned and glanced down at the floor beside the bed. Sylvie couldn't see where Samuel was lying but the look on the gunman's face chilled her. She didn't believe she had screamed and was glad, as rational thoughts began to form, she saw that the less fuss the better, for the moment at least. If the room had been invaded the results would have been disastrous. This man was a cold killer, evil and twisted, and who knew how many people would have been hurt had there been any interference from outside? She gripped the arms of the chair, not daring to speak, unable to move, though every cell in her body screamed that she must go to Samuel. She could hear and see nothing of him. It was hard to breathe and her vision was blurred with tears of fear and panic but still she held her peace, waiting, praying and hoping.

He glanced at her and grinned, raising the gun. She felt a wet patch form on her pants as her stomach flipped over and her bladder let her down. He was going to shoot her, kill her now and it would all be over. She didn't want to die, was afraid of the pain of a bullet; she had never been so terrified.

"Samuel." The whispered word brought a grin to the dark face of the thug.

"Oh, no good you trying to talk to him, no good at all. You want to see? You want to come over here and have a little look? Come on, get yourself over here and see what happens when you cross me. Come on. Now!"

She pushed herself from the chair, jelly legs threatened to betray her but she stiffened the muscles and drove herself forward. Staring straight into the eyes of the killer she staggered the few steps across the room.

Samuel lay in a red flood; it splattered across the carpet and oozed from a wound in his chest. His grey top was dark with it and it slid in a gush down his arm, dripping from his finger ends to a spreading river on the floor. His eyes were closed and a dribble of pink fluid bubbled at the corner of his lips. From where she stood it wasn't possible to determine whether he was breathing but surely the bubbles in the blood said yes.

She cried out, part scream, part sob, a sound she wouldn't have known she could make.

He laughed.

"Aw, now look, Samuel," he kicked at the motionless legs. "See how upset she is? Shall I put her out of her misery, shall I?"

Again, he turned the gun to point directly at Sylvie. She faced him square on, calm now, all feeling fled as a surreal acceptance of her fate swept through her. It was comforting, better than the panic she had felt such a short time ago. If Samuel was dead, then she didn't really care what happened any more. She had struggled and fought all her life and now if it was her fate to lose then so be it.

She took one small step forward and stretched out her hands. Wrapping her fingers around the short barrel of the gun she pulled it forward. The dark face before her twisted in puzzlement, the eyes confused. She held it to her chest, the hardness of it against her breast was something real on which to concentrate. She felt the tears running down her face and snot on her upper lip, it didn't matter, she didn't care, nothing mattered any more.

"Go on then, pull the trigger, go on, do it."

His eyes widened in excitement, she heard him draw in a breath. She was ready, calm and prepared, gripped by the emotion of the moment.

With an animal roar Samuel launched himself from the floor, blood spread and flicked from his chest and his hand as he fell on the intruder.

"No!"

The sudden change in atmosphere forced Sylvie back into the real world, the gunman staggered under the blow from a bleeding and desperate Samuel and she snatched at the barrel of the pistol and wrenched it. The damaged hand was weak and missing fingers compromised his grip. Unbelievably she had the thing. She had never shot a gun before and was unprepared for the power of the kick and the sheer shock of it all. She didn't aim, couldn't look, mustn't think but she squeezed the trigger and felt the barrel jerk upwards. His face disintegrated: blood, bone and brain spat out, showering her face and body with gore. For a long moment it seemed she would never again be able to breathe, she struggled to drag oxygen into her lungs, choking and gasping. She sucked at the air trying to stall the dizziness threatening to take her to a dark place, she couldn't go there, not yet.

The gun had fallen from her hand and lay – a lustrous piece of metal and plastic – harmless on the floral carpet.

Samuel had collapsed against the bed, the desperate effort had caused the bleeding to start anew and even as she knelt before him sobbing, his eyes began to cloud. She grasped his hands, rubbing at them, pleading with him.

"No, Samuel, no. Please, please don't die, stay with me, Samuel I love you, please don't go."

His lids flickered and his lips moved. She leaned in closer, ignoring the splatter of blood as he coughed and tried to speak.

His voice was weak and by now the noise in the hotel had reached a crescendo, someone was hammering on the room door, people were yelling and she heard the distant sound of a siren.

"Sylvie."

He closed his eyes now and she believed she could feel the vital force leave him. There came a great sigh from his ruined lungs and, sobbing inconsolably, she laid her head on his blood-soaked chest. The door burst open and in a totally different reality from that of the distraught and sobbing Sylvie, a woman screamed.

Chapter 36

Chaos and confusion swept around her. A maelstrom of noise, questions, screams and faces – dozens of faces drifted into Sylvie's field of vision, the mouths moving, sounds throbbing in her ringing ears; she made no sense of any of it. They had pushed her away from where Samuel lay and like a child she had moved to the end of the bed and sat now slumped and silent, waiting, believing he was already gone.

The police arrived and a sort of calm descended. Already two teams of paramedics were working in the confined space of the room; it was a kaleidoscope of horror. Blood was splashed over the bed, the carpets and wall, Sylvie had vomited at some stage; she vaguely remembered someone dragging her away from Samuel and leaning over, the pain in her stomach easing as she retched and heaved.

One paramedic team were simply standing back, they had known immediately that the patient they had come for didn't need them and they should leave things as they were for the police. The other team were working quietly and efficiently, a police woman stood beside them holding a plastic bag of clear fluid, a tube snaked down disappearing behind the bed. The ambulance men spoke urgently to each other, opened packs and bandages and in a tiny world apart from the rest of the room they did what they could for Samuel. So, not dead, not beyond help, maybe; she dared not hope but tried not to grieve.

In the ambulance, a police woman with a downturned mouth but kind eyes sat beside her. She clung to Samuel, just his hand, careful not to touch the needle which was poking into a vein; he didn't move, hadn't spoken. In truth she couldn't tell whether he was really alive or just breathing because they were making him breathe with their tubes and oxygen and determination.

The ride was rocky and bumpy, a reflection of the blue light on the roof of the emergency vehicle beat in time with Sylvie's heart. She could feel blood pounding through her veins, surely madness was but a beat away, she couldn't bear this, how could she bear this? The siren screamed into the night and as her hearing continued to improve, she wanted to pitch her own voice with it and scream and scream until it all stopped, until the horror went away.

At the hospital a woman in a nurse's uniform led Sylvie to a side room. The policewoman made small noises, words that crept into her brain but made no sense. They offered her tea and she didn't respond, they asked her if she was alright; the question was ludicrous, how could anything ever be alright again? She stared at them with horror-filled eyes and tears tracked unnoticed down her pale cheeks to drip onto the bloodstains on her sweatshirt.

Outside she heard muffled business, footfalls, muted voices and the occasional slam of a door. It was through a veil of unreality and she floated in it shocked to a state approaching catatonia.

The policewoman pulled her chair to a place directly in front of Sylvie's.

"We need you to be strong. They are doing what they can for your friend but we need to know what happened. We need to know who you are and who the men are who were with you. What happened in the room? Is there someone we can call, someone who can be with you now? You know, don't you, that the other man is dead? I'm sorry, was he your friend as well?"

A nurse came in with steaming cups of tea, she held Sylvie's hand, made her raise the cup to her lips and drink. The touch of skin on her own and the feel of hot sweet liquid in her mouth stirred her senses; she looked around. She had known it was the hospital, had been aware of the ambulance and Samuel, but now things snapped back into focus. She felt the cold draft from the window, the hardness of the chair and the comfort of the warm drink. She sipped again and smiled her thanks at the nurse who moved away to stand near the door. Sylvie lifted her gaze, the policewoman smiled encouragingly, noting the difference in her eyes as reality regained its hold.

"This is awful for you, what can I call you?"

"Sylvie, I'm Sylvie."

"Good, that's good. What's your surname, Sylvie?"

She didn't know what to say, she couldn't remember the name Samuel had signed them in with but surely this woman would know it, from the hotel register, or did she? Was she as kind as she seemed or was it a trap? She needed Samuel, she needed him to tell her what to do. She turned back again to the nurse.

"Samuel. What are they doing to him, is he dead?"

"He's very badly hurt, they are doing all they can. Is it your husband? Can you tell us about him, his name, can you help me to fill in the forms?"

Could she? No, she couldn't, she knew so little and yet he had said they were married. She knew only that he was a sad and grieving man who had shown her kindness. She knew he was in deep trouble and now so was she. With fresh horror she faced the fact she had killed someone, in a moment of dreadful danger and with no other choice she had fired a gun, but he was dead, his brains sprayed over the hotel room and surely she was now a murderer. This thought led onward to the next –Phil. She had been there when he had died, knew she was involved; she was in desperate trouble and she didn't know what to do.

She put down the cup and lowered her head into her hands. The nurse came back and sat beside her, wrapping warm arms around the thin shoulders, as great gulping sobs shook Sylvie's entire body. All was lost, her life was over and if, as she believed, Samuel were dying then it didn't matter anyway.

Chapter 37

"Can I see him, just for a minute, a second, can't I just see him?" The nurse just shook her head.

"I'm sorry, they have to do their work, you can see him as soon as he is stable."

"But, what if he's not, what if he is never stable, what if he dies and I haven't even been able to say goodbye? Don't you see I need to see him now, in case I can't ever see him again? Please, please."

Sylvie's small figure shook and trembled and the nurse looked in desperation at the police woman. She was young and had been sent to do the easy part, deliver tea and comfort but now she was lost. The policewoman shrugged and raised her eyebrows, she knew while Sylvie was in this state it was unlikely they could interview her successfully and in truth she did understand her need to be with her man.

"Is there no chance she could pop in, into the emergency room, just to see him?"

"I'll go and see, I'll find out anyway what is happening, OK?" She nodded in Sylvie's direction and slid through the half open door.

"Sylvie, you need to hang on, they'll do what they can. Hang on, love."

The door opened and the young nurse beckoned to them. "You can pop in for a minute, he is going for surgery but you can just see him first. There are a lot of tubes and things and of course he can't talk, he hasn't regained consciousness at all but you can see him."

She leaned over and gently patted Sylvie on her bloodstained sleeve. She had no idea of the horror this person had been through but obviously it had been extreme and if she could help a little then she felt better...

He was pale and still, tubes and wires led from beeping machines and plastic bags. The sheets were stained red, he was in a thin cotton gown. He looked vulnerable and ill, there was a tube down his throat.

"Samuel, I don't know if you can hear me, I don't suppose you can but it's me, it's Sylvie. You're going to be okay now Samuel and I'm okay. I love you. I'll be here."

They led her away, the sobbing had stopped and she was in control, the fact he was being looked after and the room had been calm had done much to reassure her.

"You can wait in the relative's room and then, afterwards, they'll probably take him to the Intensive Therapy Suite and you can pop in and see him again. Alright?"

"Yes, thank you. You're very kind, I appreciate it. Thanks."

The sky began to pale and the tiny window was filled with milky light, they had waited hours for news. The policewoman had made a couple of abortive attempts to ask questions but each time Sylvie had simply dissolved into a sobbing heap. Her seniors had called her into the corridor and she told them there was no point trying to do anything yet. They had no real idea what had happened and had no reason to take the girl in for questioning. She gave them her thoughts, not knowing that Sylvie was listening, leaning close to the gap in the door, her breath stilled, heart pounding. Now things were calmer she had begun to see that she had to act. If she was to be able to save them, she needed to come up with a story that would hold water.

Chapter 38

"I'm sorry, Sylvie, I don't understand. I thought you and Samuel were married." The detective sat on a low, upholstered chair; it had been dragged across the room to where Sylvie still perched on the hard, plastic seat. They had asked her to go with them to the police station but she refused to leave.

"I can't, I can't go anywhere. I can't leave him."

Now the detective was trying to get some information, anything at all that would help explain the horror and confusion in the hotel room. The gun had been sent away for testing and the ruined body was in the mortuary, everything picked up and packed up, swept for prints and examined for clues. They had interviewed the landlady and all she could tell them was that the young couple seemed very nice, had paid in cash and she had no idea who the other man was or how he had got into the hotel unnoticed. They hadn't forced her to confront the carnage that had been his head but she had looked at his clothes and glanced nervously at the bloodstained cloth over his face. She was tough, a Liverpool Landlady of the old school, but still she had been shaken by what had happened.

The detective leaned forward, hesitant, wanting to touch Sylvie's hand but knowing he mustn't. She was small and vulnerable, her eyes looked sore and red. They had told him she had cried and sobbed, inconsolable at times and unable to talk about what had happened. He had to encourage her; she was the only person who could help him. The doctor hadn't been too hopeful about the other man, the one now in surgery. Very serious damage to his lungs, possibly his heart, massive blood loss, shock, and so on. They didn't know what the outcome would be but the prognosis wasn't good.

So, either he was sitting with a victim or a murderer or an accessory to murder or God knew what. He tried again.

"Is Samuel your boyfriend, fiancé, what?"

"I only know I love him. We haven't been together long but, well he said we were married more as a joke, no not a joke, just so I wouldn't be embarrassed. Well you know, we didn't want any fuss, anything. Oh, I don't know, he just did."

"It's okay, I guess it happens a lot but we do need now to have things straightened out. You do see that? You're not in trouble, if you didn't do anything wrong you must tell us, all we need to do is find out what happened. Samuel can't tell us. The other man can't, so we need you to tell us. Was the other man a friend?"

This was where she would need to be careful, there was no story she could tell to show them that she was innocent.

"I don't know who he was. He was in the room when we got back from town."

"Tell you what. Let's start right at the beginning. You just tell us your name, your real name and Samuel's. We know you checked in as Mr and Mrs Percy. That's not your real name?"

She shook her head.

"Is it Samuel's name?"

She nodded; it didn't matter at the moment. His real name, Carter, was the one she must avoid. She didn't know if there were any records of him but best to err on the side of caution and as he had chosen Percy, the chance was it was safe.

"Right, so he is Samuel Percy and you are Sylvie?"

He waited, the man in the suit with his booby-trapped questions and his puzzled eyes and tired face. She stared back at him.

"Sylvie Rigby."

The little statue in the town centre had popped into her mind, the tiny lost woman. That was who she was, a lost creature, alone and friendless.

"Great, and where are you from, Sylvie?"

"Oh, all over the place, I have been in London."

"Right, good. How long have you and Samuel been together?"

As he asked the question shock thudded through her, landing in her stomach like a rock. It was so little, such a very, very short time. If she said it was barely a week they would ridicule her, it would cause more suspicion. They wouldn't understand. She didn't understand herself, how could anyone ever explain it, this attraction – it was deeper than that, a knowledge, a certainty which defied expression. Since she had gone with him to the poor shack and given him her body she had known she loved him totally. When he had said he would take her away, after the terrible thing with Phil, she had known she would go. Even though she had watched him kill the other man, seen him blood splattered and wild with violence, she wanted to be with him. How could she make them see? She couldn't, so she would lie and weave a tale, make it stick and get them out of this. She would.

"We've been together a while, I can't remember exactly how long. A while anyway. I met him in a bar. I know it sounds bad but it wasn't. I fell over and he drove me home."

Much of it was true, tiny sparks of honesty in the dark web of subterfuge. If she could keep it simple and give herself handholds of accuracy she would climb out of this mess.

"Anyway, then we got together and he brought me here. We went out, to look around the town and buy some clothes and then when we got back that man was in the room. He had a gun, he threatened us both."

"Did he shoot Samuel?"

"Yes."

"How did he get shot, the other man? There was only one gun, who shot him, Sylvie?"

Now, it was now, this was where it all came crashing down around her, the end of everything. She gulped.

"It was me, you already know don't you, it's obvious I was the one."

"That what, Sylvie? The one that what?"

Trapped, they had caught her. Her heart pounded, she couldn't breathe, her eyes had filled with tears and the room spun and tipped. She had slipped and now she was sliding deeper, there had been no choice, there were fingerprints – her fingerprints. She couldn't do this, the maze closed, there was no way to turn.

"Hey, are you okay? Put your head down. Take some deep breaths, keep calm."

Someone was touching her, she felt it distant and unreal, she was bent forward and a hand rubbed her back. The darkness receded. For a long moment she stayed where she was, gaining time, time to think. She would have to do this now, would tell them what had happened. If only her brain could keep up with her instincts, she could force it all to make sense to them and muddy the waters enough to save him.

She lifted her head.

"I'm okay, sorry I felt dizzy. I'm okay now. I shot him, the other man. I had no choice, he had already shot Samuel and he was going to kill me, he said he was going to rape me first. I thought Samuel was dead, I don't remember it very clearly but I know I shot him. I got the gun from him and I blew his face off."

As the words left her mouth, she felt a strange desire to giggle, hysteria threatened to take over; how would they react, laughing now when she had just admitted to killing a man?

She stopped, looked at their faces; there was nothing in the detective's eyes apart from a sort of resigned acceptance.

"You shouldn't really say anymore now, Sylvie. If you are telling me you shot the other man then you shouldn't say anymore, you should have someone with you, a solicitor."

"Do I have to? Can't I just tell you?"

"Wait, just wait. I need someone else in here with us, and I need you to think about what you are doing. I need to record what you say. You are going to have to come to the police station."

"I'll tell you about it now. I don't want to go away from here, not until we find out about Samuel."

"Are you sure?"

"If you let me stay until I know he's going to be alright then I'll come with you and I'll do whatever you want and I'll tell you what happened. It wasn't my fault, I had to do it."

"Stop, stop, Sylvie. Look we will stay, just until he is out of the operating theatre and then we'll go and do this properly. It's for your protection as much as anything. We have to do this the right way. For now, though, I am going to have to take your clothes. I'll go and see what I can get for you to wear. I'll leave Constable Forbes with you but I don't want you to talk to her about all of this. Okay?"

She nodded as fresh tears flooded down her face.

He couldn't help it, he felt sorry for this scrap of a girl and hoped that when she managed to tell them what had happened it would be alright for her. Had she really done whatever she had done in self-defence, from being in mortal danger? For now, he would simply try and work within the rules and play everything as straight as he could.

When the call had come in about a double shooting, he had assumed some sort of drug gang carnage. Seems he had been wrong, or maybe not, he knew enough to reserve judgement. In his mind all the time was the bag from under the bed, stuffed full of cash. This was usually a signal of drugs, but in the room there had been no other sign. Sylvie didn't look like a user and the medical bods had told him there were no drugs in Samuel's blood. It remained to be seen what was in the body of the dead man, there were scars and a deformed hand but it meant nothing to them yet.

Chapter 39

"Here you are, Sylvie, I brought you a track suit. I know it's not very glamorous but we do need to have your clothes. We will need your fingerprints as well and I'm sorry but we need a DNA sample. We can do it all later when we go down to the station but for now let's just get your clothes bagged up," the constable said.

Sylvie stretched out her hand and took the plastic wrapped parcel. Her throat was dry and there was a horrible dead feeling in the pit of her belly. This fingerprinting and processing was something she had spent so many years determined to avoid. She had been aware of it from her very early years when her father had been taken away over and over again and her mother had started the tedious business of organising representation for him and pleading his innocence, all the time in full knowledge of his guilt. So, here she was, her father's daughter, in the hands of the police, probably going to jail for a crime far more serious than any that poor useless man had ever encountered. So, it had all come to nothing.

Why had she bothered to try? All those long years fighting a past which had proved inescapable? It was hopeless, but she had to keep on trying; Samuel was fighting to live, she had to try and give him something to live for. She took a deep breath.

"Where shall I change, not here?" She indicated the little yellow room, the box of toys in the corner and the collection of picture books and old magazines. Such an innocuous little space to witness the intensity of human life that had surely passed this way. The quiet room they called it, yet surely the very walls had been imbued with the sound of lives in turmoil.

"No, no of course. Can you manage in the ladies do you think?"

"Yeah, yeah sure."

"Constable Forbes will have to go with you, sorry."

"It's fine." She dredged up a smile for them, made it seem brave and tremulous, squeezed out a tear or two.

As they stood to leave the door swung open. A doctor in his white coat and the young nurse from earlier took a couple of steps inside.

"Hi, are you, Sylvie?"

He held out his hand. She couldn't answer, desperately trying to read his expression, her eyes flicking back and forth between him and the nurse. She nodded.

"I'm Doctor Price. I've been helping to look after your husband."

"Boyfriend, he's my boyfriend."

Aware of the detective standing beside her she needed to appear honest, open.

"Oh, right, well anyway we have you as his next of kin."

Again she inclined her head. She wanted to hear, didn't want to hear; wanted this to be over but couldn't bear it to be over if the news was bad.

"Right, well. We've been struggling with Samuel; he was very badly hurt as you know. He didn't help us much." Here he smiled. Silently she hated his medical humour and understatement. She could feel nails digging into the soft

140

tissue on the palm of her hand, still she could only wait, mute with fear.

"We had to fix his lungs, he'll probably need more work later."

Her vision swum with the relief of it, *more work later, later, later.*

"He was lucky, there was very little damage to his heart from the, erm, incident itself although the shock did send him into arrest a couple of times. He seems pretty fit so he should recover well from that part. There was huge blood loss which gave us a lot of problems. Anyway, at the moment he is in recovery and then later when we're sure he's stable they'll take him to the ITU. You will be able to see him there, though don't expect too much. We're going to keep him asleep for now but you can at least pop in and see him for yourself.

The relief was too much, she knew what she should do was thank this man, thank him from the very bottom of her soul, but her throat had closed. Tears gathered there unshed, stole her ability to speak and all she could do was shake with reaction. Her knees wobbled and she had to step backwards, lower herself to the seat and hide her head in her hands.

"Are you okay?"

The nurse had laid a hand across her shoulder, bringing some human warmth.

Sylvie nodded.

"We'll leave you to calm down a bit but later on if you think of any questions just ask for me. It's been a hard night for all of us."

She heard the door swing back.

"Doctor."

"Yes."

"Thank you, I don't know how to thank you."

He didn't speak, he beamed a bright smile, nodded, and then swept out back into the real world.

"Okay, Sylvie, that's great news, really. So, when you've seen him, we can go and get started on sorting this out."

She turned to look at the detective, relief was smoothing the lines on his face, there was something else, a purpose to him, a resolve that hadn't been there before. He was ready now to take care of business. Her heart slowed, she needed to take stock and to act. It was time to plan, time to deal with this and going to the police station, answering questions, giving them cells from her body and prints from her hands might not be the way.

"Right. I'll go and get changed, shall I?" She gathered up the package of clothes and turned to the door.

Chapter 40

"I'll wait here for you." The policewoman leaned against the beige wall, she looked tired, was probably desperate for the end of her shift and some sleep.

Sylvie stepped into a small cubicle and dropped the parcel onto the closed toilet lid. There was nothing in there; some scraps of toilet paper lay on the floor. Sylvie had chosen the end one on the off chance there would be a window. There was, high up in the wall, covered on the outside with wire and with no obvious way to open it. Okay, that wasn't going to work.

She stripped off her clothes, which were stiff with dried blood.

"Do I have to take everything off, you know, my underwear and everything?"

"Yes, sorry. There should be some paper pants in the package. Sorry."

"It's okay." She had to keep this woman relaxed, friendly if possible.

Her heart was pounding, she had made a decision and it was tearing her apart. She needed to see Samuel as much as she needed to breathe but saw now it just couldn't be. After her visit to his bedside the police would take over, lead her away and then, who knew? She understood the day could end with her locked in a cell somewhere, her life taken out of her hands as the great juggernaut of the law rolled forward. They might put her in handcuffs, she had told them she shot someone so it didn't seem too far-fetched, certainly they would escort her closely. If she was to escape, then they must be taken completely by surprise.

If she had simply shot the man at the hotel – damn she still didn't even know his name – if the tale she had invented had been the truth, then she might have taken the chance and thrown her future into the hands of the authorities, but there was all the rest of it. There was Samuel's history of involvement with drugs and violence, his flight; and although she knew so little of this, she knew that being with him had tainted her. Then there was the other thing, the horrible thing with Phil. She had seen a man killed, a man she had known and shared a bed with. That Phil had been beating her was relevant at the early stage but once she left Samuel to deal with it, to hide the evidence, she had heaped trouble upon trouble and now had no idea where it left her.

Great tears followed so many others she'd already cried, tears for Samuel, for herself and for the unfairness of life. Unbelievably she had found someone to love, someone who had been kind and now she was about to leave him while he fought to live.

If she stayed, she couldn't help him, once they started the questioning it would undoubtedly make things worse. She didn't have his skill at surviving against the odds, didn't know how to lie and react to situations the way he did, though she knew she would have to learn, and quickly. Any mistakes she made could well cost him his freedom. Though it tore her apart she had to leave him, leave him and trust in his skill at survival.

She was choking now on the sorrow; her throat was tight with the pain which seemed unbearable yet must be borne. There had to be a way not only to bear it, but to act

144

now with bravery and daring and get away. What would come afterwards was lost in the mist of tomorrow.

"There are no shoes, can I keep my shoes on?"

"Oh, oh right, yeah normally they would give you slippers. Well, I don't see what else we can do, yeah keep 'em on. I suppose you've walked about so much here they wouldn't be any use to us anyway."

"Right. Okay."

Holding the bag of clothes in front of her she stepped out of the cubicle, locked a small smile on her lips, and handed the parcel over.

"Come on, Sylvie. Let's go and see Samuel and then we have to get on with this."

As they approached the elevator Sylvie began to form a plan, she had to act on instinct, take whatever fate threw her way. Constable Forbes was fairly relaxed; she was tired and trusting, she probably thought the only thing possibly on Sylvie's mind was her boyfriend behind the clouded glass doors at the end of this long corridor.

A small group of workers were waiting for the lift, Sylvie slowed her pace.

"Are you alright, Sylvie?"

"No, not really, I feel dizzy, a bit sick. I'm scared, you know, what will he look like and what's going to happen?"

"Hey, keep hold, love. We'll sort it out. Let's get this bit over and then we can get you some breakfast perhaps and a cup of tea. Look just hang on, take a minute."

"Yeah, yeah thanks."

The lift was on the floor below, coming up, the little crowd was shuffling and preparing to walk forward. Sylvie leaned against the wall, closed her eyes, listening for the doors to open. The crowd moved in, someone pushed the button, the doors began to close, she had to judge this just right, wait, wait. Now, now as the door swished the final few inches she straightened and bolted into the grey metal space.

She pushed into the group of startled people and as the slit of light closed, she had a last view of Constable Forbes darting forward, her finger extended ready to poke at the buttons, to stop the lift.

She forced a giggle from her lips. "Whew, nearly missed it, came over all dizzy again. I swear that's the last time I go on a binge. Don't know what my mum would say if I let the police take me home."

She watched their faces, lips pursed in disapproval, eyebrows raised – she had hit the right note. They had seen it so many times, silly drunken youngsters taking up precious resources week after week, never learning the lessons. They turned away from her, beneath their contempt. One young cleaner winked, and she smiled back at him.

As the doors swished open on the ground floor she flew out. Alarms were sounding somewhere, security men were scurrying forward, but for the moment confusion reigned. She sprinted across the tiles and out of the glass doors, over the pavement, jigging back and forth between taxis, pedestrians, a patient transport vehicle. She flung her head back and forth, with no idea of how to get out of the hospital grounds she simply ran along the roadway. There would be no time, no second chance, she had committed herself. Now they knew she had something more to hide than being forced to protect herself from a crazed gunman. That she had left Samuel struggling against the odds in the Intensive Care Unit would speak volumes to them, and from now they would treat her as any other fugitive criminal. She had entered the world of her father, but on a totally different level and from a different place. As she ran, she let the tears flow freely down her face, all she could do now was run as far and as fast as she could. Away, just away.

Chapter 41

Through the big stone gateposts and out onto the main road. Traffic was building up as the morning headed towards rush hour. She turned right simply because she turned right; the city was an unknown landscape and the streets a maze of shops, offices and terraced houses. She ran upwards, it was a gentle incline but an animal instinct told her to run from the dead end that was the river. She skirted round the protestant cathedral, the majesty of it lost on her. There was building work everywhere, the old city being ripped apart to make way for hope and endeavour. Her tracksuit and trainers rendered her invisible; a city where girls ran to the shops in their pyjamas and a huge percentage of the population spent their day in casual clothes, ignored a scrawny girl in sports gear.

Her heart hammered and each breath tore at her throat on and on, taking corners on a whim, turning and backtracking like the hunted creature she was, she tried to confuse the trail. Then there came a time when she couldn't run anymore. She was done, had no idea where she was or what to do next. She leaned against a grimy brick wall, bent forward and rested her hands on her thighs. Panic threatened again and she pushed it away. After a minute or so the stitch in her side eased and she raised her head. All around her cars and pedestrians forged into their days. It was too much, she had to find some peace, somewhere there had to be a place where she could curl into a ball and hide from this dreadful new reality.

She had no money, not a penny. The cheap grey tracksuit and a pair of paper knickers. That was what her life had been reduced to. She couldn't have Samuel, didn't have a family and had left her friends. What was the point of it all? She was overwhelmed with despair. For a while her brain refused to function usefully; how could this have happened, what was she going to do, what on earth was she going to do?

There was a small park up ahead, a little playground and a patch of grass, some benches. She made her way through the entrance and flopped onto the first bench. Birds sang and she was aware of the chattering and laughing of children, a couple of dogs barked. She heard it from a distance, removed and unreal, thoughts swirled unformed in her brain and her hands began to shake. She couldn't breathe now, gasping, she leaned forward.

"You alright?"

She shook her head, *go away, leave me alone, please don't make me try to speak.*

"Are you sick?"

Again she shook her head.

"Stoned, drunk, what?"

She raised her face. A tall, skinny girl stood in front of her; there was interest on her face and slight concern.

"Only if you're stoned you shouldn't stay here, the bizzies come through here."

At the mention of police Sylvie's head jerked up, she shot a look right and left.

"It's okay, don't panic, there's none now."

"I'm not stoned or drunk. I'm really tired that's all, I'm just really, really tired."

148

"Are you on the game?"

"What? No, no. I just, oh well I'm lost really and my friend is in the hospital and I don't have any money and…"

She couldn't carry on, the damned tears started again, stole her voice and left her helpless and hopeless, sobbing on the park bench with the skinny girl watching, her head tipped to one side. After a moment or two she sat down and took hold of Sylvie's hand, it was a simple, honest gesture and as Sylvie leaned towards her the stranger wrapped her arms around the heaving shoulders and patted her gently, crooning quietly.

"Aw now, come on now, it's okay, really it's okay. Come on now."

"God I'm sorry, I'm really sorry."

Sylvie pushed away making a small space between herself and the stranger who now dropped her hands into her lap and was simply smiling as she turned on the bench so she could look at this bedraggled and exhausted young woman.

"D'ya feel better? A good cry's the best thing, gets it all out."

Sylvie nodded, no she didn't feel better, didn't believe there would ever be a 'better', but this person was so very kind she didn't want to cause offence.

"Tell ya what, I was going to the cafe, get a cuppa, come on, I'll sub ya."

"No, no, it's fine. I couldn't I'm sorry I don't know what came over me."

"Where're ya from?"

"Well, down near London, but I've lived in a lot of places."

"Yeah, I could tell ya weren't from round here. Posh you are."

"Posh, me, no, no I'm not."

"Well you sound posh to me. Anyway, ya coming? Ya might as well."

She stood and dragged a short jacket tightly around thin shoulders, turned from the bench and took a couple of steps, looked back and jerked her head, an unspoken invitation. Sylvie stood up and matched her pace to the other girl's and they headed out of the park and back into the bustle of the main road.

Chapter 42

Steam clouded the windows of the little café where the air was warm with the smell of breakfast. The lanky girl stalked up to the counter.

"Two teas and two egg on toast, Phil."

The sound of the familiar name swept through Sylvie like a cold wave, she began to shiver. For a while it seemed she may faint, so she caught her lower lip tight between her teeth; she tasted metal and the small pain brought tears to her eyes but beat back the encroaching darkness.

"There ya go, food'll be ready in a bit, they'll give us a shout."

"I don't have any money; I can't pay you back."

"No, I guessed. Don't worry, I got my Giro yesterday."

The mug was heavy, thick and white and the tea was strong. The girl across the table trickled a couple of paper sachets of sugar into the liquid and stirred it round with a wooden stick.

"So, I'm Lennie."

She stretched out a thin hand. A tattoo of a snake coiled round the bony wrist and disappeared into the beige cotton sleeve of the thin jacket.

"Sylvie, thanks Lennie, I really mean it, thanks."

Tears started to her eyes again and she brushed them away with the back of her hand. Sylvie shot an embarrassed grin across the Formica towards her new friend.

"I'm sorry about all this, I've got stuff going on and to be honest I don't know what I'm going to do about it all. My boyfriend's in the hospital, he, well he got hurt, it's really bad and I feel rotten about leaving him but I didn't have any choice."

"Is it the filth?"

"No, well, actually yes. The police are looking for me but that's not all of it."

"Hang on."

Lennie unwound her lanky frame and retrieved two plates piled with toast topped with fried eggs. She slapped them down on the table, collected knives and forks from a wooden stand and then scraped her chair back in place. Sylvie was still trying to find a way to explain some of what had happened to her without risking this girl, who she knew nothing about, turning her in to the police.

For a while they ate and drank quietly, glancing at one another and sharing a smile, each a little shy now the original camaraderie of encounter had passed.

"So, your fella, what's his name?"

"Samuel, he's called Samuel."

"Is he going to be okay d'ya think?"

"I don't know, he's in intensive care, they operated on him most of the night."

"Shit girl, what ya doing here? You should be with him. Was it them slags of nurses? They can be right bitches sometimes, when me granddad was in hospital they kept telling us to leave, 'It's not visiting time, we have work to do.' Well I told 'em. 'Sod you and your work this is my granddad' and I stayed. Good job too, he died and if we'd have gone, he'd a been on his own. Not right that.

"You should go back, tell 'em you're staying. They won't throw you out, not these days, tell 'em you'll go to the papers or better still on Facebook."

"No, no the hospital people were fine, they were lovely actually. It's not that. The police were going to arrest me. I ran away, that's why I'm in this." She plucked at the thin grey top.

"Ah. Did you do it, hurt your boyfriend then?"

"No, no he was shot, not by me though, by someone else."

"Shit."

"Yeah. So, anyway I shot the man who shot Samuel. I killed him."

As she said it Sylvie felt her control slipping again, her hands began to shake, rattling the cutlery against the cheap porcelain. Lennie leaned over and took the knife and fork from her hand laying them tidily together before covering Sylvie's quivering fingers with her own warm, bony hand.

"They won't arrest you though, will they? I mean if you shot him in self-defence. You didn't do anything wrong. You should tell 'em. I'll come with you if you like, the bizzies don't bother me, they all fart in the bath just like you and me. Oh, God I'm so rude, sorry. I don't know that you do, oh that's no better." Leaning away from the table she gave a great gale of a laugh. "God, what am I like? Honestly, sorry. My mam says I should make sure my brain's in gear before I open my bloody mouth. Sorry, but I mean it, you should tell 'em. There's no need for you to have run away."

"No, no that's not all of it. There's more, so much more and I can't really tell you but it isn't as simple as it sounds. If I go back and they start to ask me questions then I know, I just know I'll get Samuel into trouble and he's spent so long, years and years just trying to keep out of it. I wish I'd never met him, I love him, God I really love him and yet I've brought him nothing but trouble right from the start and now I can't go back and I can't be with him and I don't even know if he's still alive."

The sobs would wait no longer and while the workmen and young mums and old ladies sipping their instant coffee watched with a mixture of intrigue and embarrassment, she laid her head on the table top and cried as her heart broke.

Lennie sat silently on the hard chair, now and again she lifted the mug to sip at the cooling tea. Her face was impassive but pensive, she made no move to comfort Sylvie but behaved as though having her dining companion dissolve into floods of tears was an everyday event and worthy of no more notice than she would have given a dropped chip or a spilt tube of sugar.

Chapter 43

The sobs subsided, the tears dried but she felt dead and cold inside. Tea and food had done little to lift her mood and even the sparky company of this down-to-earth young woman made no real difference.

"That feel better?"

Lennie put down her cup and watched as Sylvie blew her nose and tried to compose herself. She attempted a smile which failed miserably and gulped to head off a restart of the flood.

"I don't know what the hell to do and that's it. I have nowhere to go, not a bean, no clothes and..." She shook her head, unable to carry on.

"Tell you what, why don't you come back to mine? You can get some zeds, have a shower if you like, whatever. It's not posh my place, a bit grot really but you can come, if you like."

Sylvie began to shake her head but stilled the response, what choice did she really have? Acknowledging she knew nothing about this young woman she also had to recognise the kindness and generosity she had been shown and the terrible cul-de-sac that had trapped her. At least if she was inside, she would be less likely to come into contact with the police and an hour to evaluate her situation could only be good. She nodded.

"Thanks Lennie, it'd be great it really would."

"Come on then, might as well get going…"

* * *

The flat was small, grubby and untidy. There was one room. A bed was pushed into the corner under an old-fashioned sash window which had been dressed with flimsy pink curtains. The headboard was grey metal and pink fairy lights had been twined between the bars. The covers were thrown roughly across the mattress and a battered teddy bear glowered on the pillows. A chair and coffee table took up much of the remaining floor space with a bean bag sagging against the cream painted wall. A plastic curtain partly covered a kitchen alcove where a sink and cupboard unit stood in a dejected huddle with a small fridge. There was a door in the corner opposite the bed and Sylvie assumed this led to the bathroom. It wasn't a great space but it was warm, there were posters on the walls and a small table pushed into the corner held a mirror and a collection of bottles and tubes. Plastic boxes were pushed under the bed but there was no other storage space.

Lennie shrugged off her little jacket and hung it behind the door. An answering machine beeped urgently and she walked across to jab at the button, the screen showed six messages waiting but she made no attempt to hear them.

"Make yourself at home."

Lennie indicated the chair with a sweep of her hand and then turned away. She straightened the kitchen curtain, pushed the bean bag further into the corner with her foot and fiddled with a couple of the bottles on the table. She seemed twitchy and ill at ease, Sylvie felt a tension rising that hadn't been there before. She had made a mistake, she shouldn't have come.

"Look Lennie, I'm really grateful, I am, you've been brilliant but I think I'd better go, see if I can get back to the hotel, maybe I can get my stuff."

She knew it was a ridiculous thought, everything would surely have been taken away but it seemed like a good reason to leave.

"I might be able to, you know, go to the bank, I have a bit of money, if I tell them I lost my cards." She shrugged.

Lennie turned to look at her, a tear glinted in the corner of her eyes, her face was drawn and sad.

"I'm sorry, Sylvie, honestly I had no choice about this. I don't wish you any harm but I didn't have any choice."

As her face creased in puzzlement alarm wormed its way into Sylvie's gut. What was this?

A sharp slam and the sound of feet on the bare wood of the staircase notched up her sense of alarm. The door flung back and two men in dark jackets and jeans filled the space. They strode into the room ignoring Lennie who had backed against the wall, her hand pressed to her mouth, tears now dripping across her cheeks. She shook her head as her eyes sought out Sylvie, sending a wordless message of despair and shame across the meagre space.

Sylvie had backed as far as she could into the corner. Her legs were tight against the frame of the bed. She bent her knees and shuffled backwards without looking onto the bundled covers. The two figures crossed the room before she had the chance to do more than simply drag herself as far into the corner as she could. There was no escape.

"I'm sorry, I'm sorry." Lennie was sobbing, crouched in the corner her skinny knees drawn up in front of her chest. As the two intruders grabbed Sylvie and lifted her bodily, squirming and wailing, Lennie buried her head behind her arms and sniffled quietly to herself.

"Piss off, let me go. Christ let me go. What are you doing? Who the hell are you? Help me, Lennie, help me."

There was no help. With a rough hand pressed across her face to quieten her and lifted from her feet Sylvie was hustled down the narrow staircase. Once outside they threw her across the back seat of the black four-wheel drive which had been parked on the yellow lines outside the building.

"Shut up bitch, shut up or I'll shut you up. Stay down, keep quiet."

The door slammed. No way was she keeping quiet, Sylvie scrambled to kneel on the seat and hammered on the tinted glass of the windows.

"Help me, help me someone. For God's sake help me. Lennie, Lennie. Shit, somebody help me."

She didn't see the blow coming, she felt the jolt as her head was jerked violently to the side; she felt her lip split and the spurt of blood and then there was nothing. She slid to the floor of the big car, her arms and legs a tangle in the confined space. The man who had hit her threw a tartan blanket on top of the bundled body, slammed the door and climbed in beside his mate who was already indicating and drawing away to join the stream of traffic.

Chapter 44

Waves of nausea marked her return to consciousness; Sylvie rolled instinctively to her side as her mouth filled with saliva. A spew of vomit splashed onto the grey concrete floor. Her stomach heaved again. Slime covered the side of her face and slipped under her hand as she tried to push away, the stink of it was sour and vile in her nostrils. Her eyes streamed with reaction to the pain, the vomiting and the terrible nameless fear. She groaned.

"Shut up."

She was cold, shivering convulsively, her head pounded and her throat felt raw. She lay back wanting the darkness to carry her away again, this was too much now. It was time for it to be over, she was desperate to make it end.

A push against her side moved her; she tried to roll away from the jabbing foot.

"Get out of your muck, bitch. Come on you've had long enough feeling sorry for yourself. Shift."

When she opened her eyes this time the walls held still. She moved her head, peering into the gloom. This was a big space, it wasn't possible to see the edges of the room. The roof was high above; she saw steel girders and dim grey windows.

Now, better able to take stock, it was clear the pain was mostly in her head and neck. The rest of her body seemed relatively unhurt though her feet were numb and cold. She shuffled and squirmed, dragging herself into a sitting position. Her knees were bent and by holding onto them with her hands clasped she was fairly steady. A rope around her ankles was threaded through a ring set into the concrete floor. She could feel him near, the man who had spoken, but couldn't see him. As she tried to turn rough hands grabbed the sides of her head.

"Enough, keep still now. Keep very still, face forwards. Do as I tell you, don't you dare turn round."

Sylvie gulped, tears flowed. She sniffed and mopped her face with the sleeve of the nasty grey top. Despair overwhelmed her, she had no idea where she was, who she was with or what they wanted from her.

Lennie, why? The memory of those haunted, guilty eyes came to her. Sylvie knew only too well how life would push and pummel until you did unspeakable acts. She tried to push these thoughts away, there was no space in her mind now for anger, all that mattered was survival, possibly, or at least for this to finish quickly. Now her mind filled with only the wish that the end would be swift because surely this could only go one way. She prepared to die.

He was very close now; she felt his presence, his breath on her neck and the heat from his body. She was plunged back into darkness, a physical darkness this time. She couldn't breathe, her nose and mouth were blocked, there was roughness against her face; she couldn't tell whether her eyes were open or closed. A sack or a cloth, something was over her head and his hands were at her neck, a noose tightening, tightening. Another scream rose in her throat but horror stole it, rendering her dumb. He would strangle her now, or hang her. She squirmed against his grip, flailing blindly in the dark till her hands were snatched back and sharp pain in her wrists told her they were tied.

Now there was movement around her ankles, clawing fingers, pulling and scratching. The ropes were loosed. She kicked uselessly against the weight of him leaning on her legs.

His hand groped and fumbled around her waist. His nails rasped on the delicate skin as he tore away the cheap trousers. She heard him laugh as the paper pants were ripped away.

"Nice, classy."

"No, no, please don't, please don't."

Her pleas rippled in the silence, as the knowledge of what was happening crawled into her brain.

He struck her then, through the sacking. Her face hit the concrete with a dull smack. More hands now, other hands, gripping her legs pulling them, stretching them apart. Still she screamed, and she fought.

"Hold her, Si, keep her still."

"Don't please. No."

There was no way to fight, there was nothing but to try and bear it, the pain and the fear and the horror as he grabbed at the tops of her legs, thrust his fingers roughly into her body. Then as her insides blazed with agony, she felt him pushing inside her, thrusting, tearing and destroying…

It was over, she felt him stiffen and moments later he rolled away with a grunt. She was numbed, appalled, disgusted and swept with misery.

"Hold her, grab her legs. Shift over, Mo, my turn."

Her struggles now were feeble, what was there left to fight for? She simply lay on the cold floor as tears trickled across her face and she lost herself in the world of pain. Now the other man took his turn, he wanted fight, something to fulfil his need to overwhelm her. He slapped at her face, dragging the sack upward till it covered only her eyes, he grabbed at her cheeks and twisted and pinched at the tender flesh.

"Slut, whore, you don't even fight."

He thrust himself inside her harder and harder, "You like this bitch, like it do ya? Shall I give you something more to like?"

His great hand closed round her throat, she choked and gagged, bucking and squirming as her lungs cried out for oxygen. Surely he was killing her now. Silently she prayed, please, please let me die, make it stop. Still he pounded into her body; her back rasped and scraped on the concrete, her head was bursting, and now she could take no more. It was unendurable and her brain shut down, taking her out, back to the dark.

Chapter 45

The nightmare wouldn't go away, Sylvie tried to escape the pain and fear but it held her fast. Her arms and legs refused to react, she was shivering uncontrollably, her teeth hammered in her mouth and damp clothes clung to her shaking body.

Inside she was raw. Red heat assaulted her belly, she felt fluid between her legs and whenever she moved a gush of warmth told her all was not well.

Thunder pounded in her head and her face felt puffy and unreal. She kept her eyes closed – once she forced the lids open it would be time to acknowledge the reality of her situation.

Eventually and inevitably it was time to come back. The seat was hard and her hands were fixed behind it. Her shoulders had gone past pain to numbness, her ankles were tied. There was something locking her lips together and the chattering of her teeth cut and rubbed at the inside of her mouth. The agony in the base of her stomach was the worst thing and was without doubt the site of most damage. She hoped it was huge and soon it would take her away; she wanted to die now, this was dark and dreadful, too terrible to be borne.

Life wouldn't leave her, her body forced her to endure, so, through the pain and fear and despair, she climbed back to consciousness. It was fully dark now, she heard no-one near though her ears stretched in the silence seeking the sound of breathing, the scrape of shoes on concrete or the mutter of voices.

She heard moaning, a quiet pitiful sound and it was only when she realised it came from her own throat that it ceased.

The knowledge that she was truly alone came to her slowly through the veil of helplessness. She shuffled on the hard chair, her hands were tied but not tightly, with small movement she felt the binds begin to ease. She pulled and tensed and wriggled and in the midst of a dreadful pain was able to free her arms and pull them forward. She sat cradling her abdomen and sobbing into the darkness. In the end she had to acknowledge she lived, and living required her to act and so bending forward, grunting with the agony, she was able to untie her ankles and then to rip the tape from her face. Her eyes found the paper, left in front of the chair. Once she was free, she reached and picked up the note.

> *Take your stinking body back to your boyfriend. Tell him that we are watching, we are always watching and we are coming. He is ours. He is a dead man walking.*

The venom behind the words drew little reaction, her body was ruined, her soul was scorched, mere ink on paper moved her not at all. She folded the white sheet over and over in her bloodied hands and then tucked it into the end of her sleeve.

Her legs and lower body were bare and covered in blood and bruises. She whimpered whenever she moved but knew she must. The pants were ripped beyond all redemption, the grey top fell short of the top of her thighs covering most of her stomach but not much of her bottom. She was alone, she had no clothes, she was hurt, so very hurt and had no idea where she was. A tiny gasp escaped her mouth "Samuel". He couldn't help her; she didn't even know if he was still alive and the mere sound of his name drew hot tears from her sore eyes. She had returned to the chair and now rocking back and forth gave herself up to the grief. Why not cry, surely she had earned the right to cry and never stop?

"Sylvie, Sylvie. Is it you? Don't be scared, it's me, it's Lennie."

The silhouette moved and shifted, coming across the concrete, tall and skinny, nervous and jumpy but getting nearer.

"It's me, God Sylvie, are you alright?"

"No."

The single word was faint and pathetic.

"I'm here to help you, they called me. They said you were waiting; told me I should come and get you. Are you hurt?"

"Yes, yes I'm hurt."

Now Lennie had moved close enough to see for herself the damage to the other girl. Her eyes flooded with tears of shock and pity.

"Oh God, Sylvie. I'm so sorry. Christ what did they do?"

She knelt now before the chair and wrapped her arms around the small, shuddering figure.

"Ssshh. Shhh."

She shrugged off her jacket and wrapped it around Sylvie's shoulders.

"Wait, wait. I've got a blanket in the car. I'll get it."

Sylvie reached out and snatched at the skinny hand.

"No, don't leave me. Take me with you, take me. Help me to stand."

They wobbled across the great space towards the sliding warehouse door and then, with Sylvie on the verge of collapse, Lennie pushed her into the back of a battered and rusted old car. She tucked a soft blanket around her, tears dripping onto the colourful pile, crooning on and on as Sylvie laid back and gave herself up again to darkness.

Chapter 46

"I've run a bath, I put some antiseptic stuff in it. I think you should go to the hospital though; you're bleeding and you look really bad."

"No, no. I can't. They'll call the police; I know they will. Just let me get clean, let me have a bath."

The room was small, dark and dingy; the pink wall tiles were rimmed with mould and the taps had long since lost their shine, but the water was hot and the radiator held a big pink towel warming ready for her. With gasps of pain Sylvie lowered herself into the warm tub. The water turned to pink as the blood washed into it, she felt a wave of nausea but turned her face away. It was as if her body was ingrained with filth and would never be clean again. She could feel the ghost of his hands, on her ankles, around her waist and the tops of her legs. The soreness in her vagina and all around the area from tears and bruising was beyond belief and though she had refused the hospital, her body was telling her there was damage deep inside. She would have to trust in fate that it would heal and there wouldn't be permanent harm. Her arms and legs were scratched and reddened from the rough treatment and the bindings, her face was sore from the beatings and her heart was broken from it all.

There was a knock on the door. "Are you okay, do you need anything?"

She couldn't let Lennie look at her, the darkness at the warehouse had hidden her shame and the blanket in the car had wrapped her round. She looked now at her battered body, which she couldn't bear to let anyone else see.

"I'm okay I think, I'll be okay. Do you have any aspirin and any underwear, maybe a sanitary towel?"

"Yes, of course, I've got a dressing gown for you and I've turned the electric blanket on. You need to get into bed. I put some soup on, it's only tinned but it'll make you feel better. Well, I think it might."

The kindness reduced Sylvie to fresh tears and she let them flow, a salve to her soul as the water soothed and gentled her physical self.

* * *

Wrapped in a soft dressing gown and snuggled under the duvet she sipped at a mug of soup. Lennie had hardly spoken, but she held the bedding as Sylvie slipped underneath and then tucked a towel over the covers before handing her the soup. She gingerly perched on the edge of the bed.

"God, Sylvie, what can I say? I am sorry, so very sorry. If I'd known what they would do, if I'd had any idea, I wouldn't have brought you back here. I would never."

"Did you know? All the time in the park and the café, did you know who I was and how they wanted me?"

"Yes, well some stuff, what they told me. They brought me there, pointed you out. They told me you'd nicked some gear from 'em. Sylvie, I know it's no excuse but I owe 'em. Big time, I owe 'em and they said if I brought you back here, they'd let me off some of it. I thought if you'd nicked some stuff, well you'd be hard, able to look after yourself. Then when I got talking to ya and saw you weren't like that I was in too deep; I couldn't get out. They were watching us all the time and they followed us back and God, I didn't want to do it but I couldn't get out of it."

She buried her head in her hands and sobbed, "I'm so, so sorry. I thought they'd just give you a bit of a belting and we've all had them, haven't we? I never thought they'd do this, all this."

"Couldn't you have warned me, at least given me some sort of sign? Okay, you were in trouble I see that but you could have tried to let me know." The other girl shook her head, unable to speak. "I thought they were going to kill me, I almost wished they would. I've been with some rough blokes but this, I don't know how you get over this."

Lennie lifted her face but had no words that could help to ease the hurt that had been caused or to lessen the shame that she felt, so she slumped dejected and silent on the edge of the bed.

"Look." Sylvie held out the folded note and watched as Lennie read it.

"Christ, they mean to kill him, don't they?"

"I suppose they think he shot the other bloke. There's other stuff as well from before. He's been running from them for years and he was doing okay until he got mixed up with me. I don't know what to do now. I have to help him. How are you mixed up with them, Lennie? Do you do drugs?"

"Me, no. Not any more, I did once but not now, I'm clean."

"So, why do you owe them?"

"Hmm, it was for Brian, my brother. He's dead now but before he died, I got him some stuff and I didn't pay 'em and…"

"That's horrible, I'm sorry about that, about your brother," Sylvie said.

Lennie nodded. "Yeah, well he couldn't help himself. He tried a few times, to get clean, went on the Methadone programme, all sorts of stuff but no, he didn't make it in the end."

The statement was bald, almost devoid of sentiment; this girl had been through much and survived – like Sylvie herself. A kindred spirit. As the thought began to take root it was followed by another and Sylvie felt the anger start to rise and with it a desire for vengeance.

For now, though, the warmth, the relative safety and reaction to the trauma of the last hours overwhelmed her and she allowed herself to drift away.

Lennie looked down at this poor creature, guilt and sadness swept her and then she felt the anger start to simmer.

Chapter 47

Here it was – the rest of her life. Sylvie knew she was changed forever. It wasn't that innocence had been lost, God knew she'd been long past innocence, but deep inside a dark place had been created. It was, she knew, a place of hate and for now she let it sit. She believed she had a right to hate; she also vowed to take revenge.

Lennie brought her tea and toast. The girl looked haunted, her eyes were teary and her face pale save where dark smudges witnessed the sleeplessness of the past night. She plumped pillows, tucked the covers and squeezed Sylvie's hand.

"How is it?"

"Bloody sore, all over. I think the bleeding might have stopped though. I can hardly move. Shit."

"Can I help?"

"No, no it's okay just let me sit up."

"Just stay where you are today, stay in bed. I have to go out later but you'll be alright here. At least I think you will."

Sylvie shook her head. "I can't, I have to get away from here. They know where I am, I'm scared stiff they'll come back. I don't know where I'm gonna go but I have to get away.

"Lennie, I'm sorry about what I said," she continued. "I sort of understand; I see that you didn't have much choice. You've been good to me; it's not your fault."

The short speech reduced the other woman to yet more tears but she smiled in spite of them and leaned in to hug Sylvie gently.

"Well, it feels like my fault, I can't believe I let it happen. Bloody scum." Lennie shook her head and rubbed her hands over her face. "So, what are you gonna do?"

"I can't go to the police. I can't go back to the hospital or the hotel. I really need to know how Samuel is and I need to get some money."

"Can you use the internet, transfer money from your account?"

"Yeah, if I can remember my password," Sylvie replied.

"Well, if you like you can transfer it to mine and I can get some out for you. I can only get a hundred pounds a day but I can get some today and some tomorrow, will that work?"

"That'd be great, it really would. I need some clothes."

"Well, I have some stuff but it won't really fit you, you're welcome to anything but if you'd rather, I can go and get some for you. I can get it on my card and then you can pay me back. Shit, I feel bad asking you to pay me back but..." She shrugged.

"No, no that'd be great. I need everything, would you mind?"

"I'll go now. Tell me what you want, your size and stuff, and you have another bath if you like."

They hugged again and Lennie dragged on her jacket. "My computer's on, over there and you can log on, I piggyback on the bloke downstairs' wifi. He doesn't mind."

* * *

172

The outside door slammed and Sylvie jerked from her half-dream, scuttered in panic to the bathroom and fumbled with the door lock. She leaned against the wood breathing rapidly, her heart pounding against her ribs. She knew she couldn't stay here, and would have no peace of mind in this place where she was vulnerable.

"Sylvie, Syl. It's me, Lennie. I'm on my own, it's okay, are you in the bog?"

Lennie stood in the middle of the room her hands full of plastic bags, a concerned look on her face.

"I thought you'd gone."

"Sorry, Lennie, I'm just jumpy you know."

"Course you are. Anyway, look, I got some stuff; I hope it's okay for you. I got some money as well, did you manage to do the bank stuff?

"No, you didn't leave me your account details."

"What am I like? Right, here, you look at the stuff, I can take any of it back if you don't like it. I just went to the ordinary shops for most of it. It's cheap stuff, M&S for the undies though. I don't know what you usually do."

"Oh, it'll be great. Just to have something of my own'll be great."

"Right, you get dressed, I'll put the kettle on and make us a butty."

"Sorry?"

"A butty, you know – a sarnie. I hope ham's okay, I got cheese as well."

"Oh, oh right. Yeah great. Then we'll do the bank and then, will you do me a favour?"

"'Course I will anything."

"Will you ring the hospital for me? See if you can find anything out about Samuel."

"Yeah, but they probably won't tell me anything. I had an idea though. My aunty is a cleaner there, I could ask her to see if she can find out anything."

"Will she be okay? It won't put her in any danger or anything? The police are there. At least I suppose they still are."

"It's fine. Look, let me ring her now, I think she'll still be in work. You have a look at the clothes."

Sylvie came out of the bathroom where she had taken the plastic bags. Jeans, top, socks and trainers, simple things but they made such a difference, she felt human again, almost normal. On the outside.

Lennie was busy in the kitchen alcove buttering rolls and slicing cheese. She turned as she heard the bathroom door closing.

"Oh, they're great. Are you happy with it all?"

"Yeah, they're fine, thanks. You even thought to get me spare socks and knickers. How much do I owe you?"

"The receipts are there, I tried to keep it reasonable. You can just transfer some money into my account and then I'll take out the difference in cash from the hole in the wall. Like I said I hate to ask you for money, I feel so guilty, but, well, you know."

"Yeah, I know and anyway I wouldn't feel right not paying for the stuff. Did you ring your Aunty?"

"I did. She's in work this affie, she's going to try and find out what she can. It might not be much but, well, we'll have to wait and see. She's great she'll do her best," Lennie said. "Here ya go, sarnie's ready, do you want tea or coffee?"

"Coffee'd be great thanks."

And so they sat, like any two friends meeting for lunch. Two friends with so much drama between them that it made cheese sandwiches and coffee ludicrous, but what choice did they have? At the end of the day the minutiae of life soothe the spiky edges and calms the tormented waters.

Chapter 48

Lennie stood looking down at the slight form of her visitor. Curled under the duvet with her bruised face barely visible and her hair spread over the pillow, she looked like a child. A child who had been to hell. She leaned forward and gently shook Sylvie awake.

"Hi, have you had a nice nap? How're you feeling?"

"Yeah, shattered to be honest. God, I'm sore all over again; I'm stiff and my face hurts." Suddenly, out of the blue Sylvie began to shake; she buried her face in her hands, sobbing.

"Hey, hey what's matter? Come on, come on you're okay, I'm here."

Lennie wrapped her skinny arms around the trembling form – it was all she could do. Eventually, the crying abated and Sylvie looked up; her face was drawn with despair.

"I'm sorry, sorry. It's just that every now and again it all comes back, whap and I'm back there. A great sweep of blackness, it's so scary. I can't believe it. Why, why did this happen to me?"

There was no answer and Lennie simply sat cradling her new friend and fought internally with the guilt.

"I'll make a drink. Are you okay now? How's the pain in your stomach?"

"It's horrible but I think it's better than it was. Oh, did you hear from your Aunty?" Sylvie asked.

"Hmm."

Sylvie could see from the clouding of Lennie's eyes that there was something wrong. Her stomach flipped, she couldn't get the words out, so, in the end, simply stared at the other woman willing her to know there are some questions just too difficult to verbalise."

"She rang me while you were asleep. She went up to the intensive care place. The police are still there, of course. Anyway, she has a couple of mates working up there."

Playing for time so obviously, but Sylvie went along with it steeling herself, wanting to know but fearing the worst.

"It's not good. I'm sorry."

As the tears began to fall Lennie came back to the bed and perched beside the hunched figure.

"He's not dead though, is he? Tell me now. He's not dead?"

Lennie shook her head. "No, he's not dead. He's not good though. He's had two more cardiac arrests; he's had to go back to the operating theatre and they don't know what's going to happen. They don't know if he'll wake up again."

"What do you mean they don't know?"

"Well, at first he was in a coma because they wanted him to be. Now though, he's just in a coma and they don't know if he'll ever come round or…"

"Or what?" Her fingers were coiled now around Lennie's skinny arm, the knuckles white. "Or what?"

"Well, he might just stay like that for a long, long time. Or…" She shrugged, trying to convey the rest of the information without having to speak.

"Or he might die?"

"Yes, they think he might die," Lennie said. "Of course, this is only one of the nurses, the doctors wouldn't tell a cleaner anything but this girl is a mate of my cousin."

Irrelevant information filling the great sad void and she knew it wasn't working. Inside the flat now there were many moments of silence. The noise from the road, the shouts of children and revving of cars were a part of another world, where people weren't fighting for their lives or struggling to come to terms with a hideous assault on their bodies and their souls. The other world, sanity and normality. How very far away it was from this scruffy little room and these two grieving women.

After a while Sylvie stirred, she stood up and slowly straightened, pain and resolve visible in her movements.

"Can she get me in?"

"In?"

"Yes, your aunty, can she get me in to the hospital?"

"I don't know. I suppose. Well maybe. I could ask. But the police are still there, they have a bloke on a chair outside his room and the others keep coming to see how he's doing. You can't go back, they'll have you."

"It doesn't matter. I don't care. I want to see him and that's all. If he's going to die I don't care what happens to me and if he is going to… die… you know, then I want to see him first. Ask her, will you ask her if she can get me in?"

"Yes, she isn't back until tomorrow morning, it'd look funny if she went in now but I'll ask her, if you're sure. They might grab you though, and even if she gets you in to the department, I don't know how you'd get into his room. No, it's daft, a daft idea."

"Please, ask her. I won't get her into trouble or anything I promise. As soon as she gets me into the hospital, I'll leave her. Ask her." Sylvie held out the mobile phone…

"Right that's it. She'll come in the morning, she'll bring a spare uniform and get you in by the back door. She doesn't know how you'll get in though; she said the bizzies are all over the place."

"It's okay. I just want to try and if I don't, then so be it but if I don't give it a go and he dies, I'll never forgive myself. Anyway, what the hell else is there for me to do?"

Lennie heaved a great sigh. "Listen, I asked a mate if you could go there for tonight, because you were scared here. Actually, though, I think it's okay, they'll have gone now, you know. They never hang around for long, they have a bloke at the hospital but he's a muppet, I think he must be somebody's brother and you shouldn't have a problem with him, if you wear the uniform. Si and Mo will be gone for now till they think Samuel is coming round or whatever."

"Is that their names then, Si and Mo? I didn't know," Sylvie asked. "I'd rather stay with you to be honest. If you think I'm safe here. Actually, I don't much care anymore. All I want now is to see Samuel and then I just don't give a shit."

Chapter 49

Samuel was lost in the pain, it was deep and profound; it consumed him. Confusion and panic gripped him, he was choking, something clutched at his throat. He tried to scream, it was impossible – he had no voice, was he drowning? He must be drowning, surely. His arms and legs refused to move – tethered; he was tethered. Sudden bright light speared his eyes. His ears hummed and sang, the world was a violent place and so he fought it. Choking, bucking and writhing and grasping at the monsters holding him.

The baby was beautiful; he always knew it would be. With a mother like Marie how could it have been any other way? She was smiling at him now, glowing with pride and happiness. She was but a step away, holding out the child, now he would cradle his son, he reached for the tiny bundle. Marie stepped back. *No, let me hold him, please, let me hold him, come here Marie, bring him to me.* She stepped away again, her eyes glittered with emotion. She raised a hand, blew a kiss and then she left him again, and as before, she took their child with her.

"It's alright. You're okay, don't struggle." The voice came from far away, "We're going to let you have a sleep, it will all be better when you wake up. Don't worry. We are looking after you."

It made no sense, he was terrified, he wanted Marie. She had gone into the dark. His limbs became leaden, the panic abated, and he floated into the welcoming void.

The brightness was painful but the panic had gone. He felt calm but puzzled, there was still a strange feeling in his throat, he tried to swallow and it brought back the pain and some panic.

"It's alright, Samuel, don't be upset. You have a tube in your throat, it's to help you to breathe, just relax, you mustn't try to talk."

A face floated into his line of vision, a kind face smiling at him. He felt a hand, soft on his face. The world was returning, he tried to look around.

"Don't move too much, Samuel. I know you're confused but just keep quiet and it'll all make sense soon. You were hurt. You've been very ill but you're going to be fine. Do you understand me? Just squeeze my hand."

The other hand in his palm was an anchor, and he squeezed, feeling the movement in his own fingers, in his arm.

"That's great. Now you have to be patient. You had some damage to your lungs and you've been very poorly. We have to make sure you can breathe on your own before we take the tube out. I know it's not very nice but it shouldn't be for long. Okay?"

He squeezed again and the nurse, he recognised now it was a nurse, smiled at him.

"Brilliant. Now we are here with you, we aren't going to leave you on your own, if you want anything you'll have to point. You have a catheter to take care of your bladder and there are tubes in your arm for fluid. The doctor is on his way and he'll give you a once over. Okay love?"

He squeezed.

Slowly it made some sense, he was in hospital, he couldn't remember how but the nurse would tell him, or the doctor. His throat felt odd and he was sore, his chest felt really painful and his whole body ached. He tried to remember but nothing came except that Marie had been there. He wondered where she was now; poor Marie, she'd be so worried. He wanted to hold her hand, he wanted to tell her he was okay. He tried to attract the nurse, raised his hand, tried to wave and she saw him and came to the bedside.

"It's okay, Samuel, just keep calm. Do you need something?"

He nodded. She stroked his arm and looked around, checked his catheter, his pillow and the sheet covering him. She reached over and pulled a little notepad from the top of the trolley beside the bed. She handed it to him and snapped the pen from her pocket.

"Do you think you can write it down for me?"

He took the pen and struggled with the incredible weight of it, his fingers had forgotten how to make the shapes, she steadied his hand. "Marie," he wrote.

When she read the word the nurse simply shook her head. Your friend, she isn't here. Don't worry about it now, just try to relax.

He didn't understand, there was so much he didn't understand, but Marie, she wouldn't leave him, not now. Where was she? Tears formed in his eyes, he needed her so badly. The nurse took his hand and stroked his head.

"You've been through the mill, Samuel, don't upset yourself, give it time just try to keep calm."

He felt his lids starting to close, he was so tired but Marie, where was she? He needed to see her, why wasn't she here?

Chapter 50

"Come on love, we have to go in this way, then I have to clock in. Just stay near me and nobody'll notice you," Lennie's aunty said.

Sylvie was dressed in a blue overall and carried a plastic shopping bag, underneath she wore the plain clothes Lennie had brought. She fit in well with the other cleaners and maintenance people jostling and joking as they passed through the scratched and battered door at the rear of the huge hospital building. A couple of the workers grinned at her.

"This another of your nieces, eh Marj?"

"Yeah, that's it, she's starting today and you keep your hands off her, Steve. I don't want you leading her astray."

They were inside and as they made their way through the narrow corridors Marj pulled Sylvie into a small alcove.

"Right, now, if you're still sure you want to try this you just need to go up those stairs. Four flights gets you to the back entrance of the ITU. I don't think there's a copper there but once you get inside there are a couple on duty all the time as far as I can tell. You might be able to sneak in. There are some baskets, you need to take a flimsy overall, some overshoes and a hat. Use the hand cleaning thing on the wall and then it's up to you whether you can blag your way into his room or not. I don't think you'll be able to do it but…" She gave a shrug and shook her head.

Sylvie gave the other woman a quick hug.

"Thanks, Marj, and please don't worry, if I get caught I'll never mention you, I promise."

She took the stairs slowly, her body still reminded her of the events in the warehouse and she was nervous anyway. She was frightened she would end this venture in the police cells and all the horror of the past days would have been for nothing. However, she was driven by the need to see him and the knowledge that Samuel was a countable number of steps away.

The door was painted blue, a small window in the side just above the handle gave a view of the department. Letters had been stencilled onto the wood 'ITU'. Beside the door there was a small dispenser with a laminated notice exhorting her to wash her hands. Plastic crates held packages containing the flimsy overalls, the overshoes and paper hats. She gowned up and squeezed the antiseptic gel onto her hands. The door was heavy and she squared her shoulders as she pushed at it. It refused to move. She pushed again then saw the small metal box, "Please Ring and Wait". As Sylvie jabbed at the button, a nurse stationed behind a central desk turned to look in her direction and then came and dragged open the door.

"Cleaner, sorry I'm new – I was told to come here."

"Didn't they give you a pass key?"

Sylvie shook her head.

"Honestly, bloody contractors."

With this remark the nurse turned on her heel and stalked back across the vinyl flooring, she turned and looked over her shoulder.

"Cleaning stuff's in the cupboard, don't suppose they told you that either, did they?"

Sylvie lowered her gaze and trod quietly past the desk and slipped into the little room. She leaned against the wall for a moment giving her pounding heart the chance to settle and calm. The room was filled with shelving units holding boxes and bottles, there were mops in the corner and a vacuum cleaner.

She had glanced around and as Marj had warned her, a policeman in uniform sat on a plastic chair outside what must be Samuel's room. The door was closed and there was no way to tell who was in there. She doubted he would be alone but had no real knowledge of how this all worked. Most of the other patients were in beds in the main unit and easily visible to the staff. If Samuel was in the side room then surely there would be someone with him, either police or hospital workers or possibly even both.

She collected the vacuum cleaner and made her way back through the department. Plugged in and turned on it became a screen and a shield, she was the cleaner. Inch by inch she swept her way towards his door.

She was relieved that the policeman on duty was one she hadn't met before. He looked up and gave her a disinterested smile and then went back to his study of a magazine. She continued with her vacuuming.

She laid her hand on the door handle and instantly the constable was alert.

"No love not in there."

"Oh, but I have to clean all the floors. It's what they said, all the floors, behind the desk, inside the storage rooms everything."

"That's not a storage room, there's a patient in there."

"Oh, well I'll be quiet. Try not to disturb them. Are they really sick then? Is that why the door's shut? Is it a bloke or a woman?"

"Look love, I told you not in there. Now just get on with whatever else you have to do, right?"

He glared at her now and she turned away with a shrug and continued until the whole unit had been covered. Then she went and brought out the toilet cleaning equipment. She was winging it now but he was so near. If she could just see him it would be enough, she didn't even need to talk.

She cleaned the toilets in the main unit and as she passed the closed door she stopped.

"Now I have to do the bog in there. Even you can see that, it's a hygiene thing, the bog needs to be done. I won't be long. Come on please, I'm on probation, I need to show 'em I can do a good job."

The policeman gave her a long look, glanced down at the pail of cleaning gear and shrugged his shoulders.

"Go on then, quick mind and I'm standing by the door. Don't disturb the bloke and don't try to talk to him and bloody well hurry up. My boss'll be here in five minutes and he'll have my guts for garters if he finds you in there."

She pushed open the door.

Chapter 51

Back in the shabby flat, Lennie paced back and forth. She stubbed out a cigarette, plopped down onto the chair but couldn't settle. Her mind whirled. Although their friendship was in its infancy she felt strongly drawn to Sylvie. She recognised in the other girl things which were part of her own make up. Though they hadn't talked about it, she knew Sylvie had been down many of the same roads she herself had travelled.

Life had been tough, a struggle from the earliest days. Losing her brother to drugs, her own soul to prostitution and many friends to crime, depression and all the other things that blighted lives around her, she had simply trudged on taking where she could and giving when it was possible. Now though, after seeing the dreadful injuries and the depth of terror in her eyes in the warehouse, she was tormented by what had happened to Sylvie.

Though Sylvie had told her repeatedly that she didn't blame her, Lennie held herself totally responsible and though she could forgive her brother for wasting his life and herself for many of the things she had done, this was now too much. She had done it because she was afraid, truly afraid for her own life but it was no longer enough to use fear as an excuse, she had to take control. A plan began to form.

When Sylvie came back from the hospital, she needed to talk to her, put her ideas into words, and she hoped to be able to convince the other girl it was the way to go. She lit another cigarette and for the hundredth time in the last hour checked the clock. Time crawled by, it was only mid-morning. She threw on her jacket and went out for a walk. She would go to the pub, find some company and try to pass the day.

As she made her way towards the short cut through the little park, she didn't notice the big black car parked around the corner, or the two thugs waiting and watching.

* * *

Back at the hospital Sylvie took a breath as she pushed open the door to Samuel's room. It was dimmer in here than the department as a whole, blinds had been pulled over the window. A nurse sat in the corner on a small easy chair and she glanced up as Sylvie slid through the door.

"What are you doing? You can't come in here."

"Cleaner, I just need to clean the toilet."

As she spoke, she took another tentative step. Her eyes were beyond her control, they swung of their own accord towards the bed. He was propped on several pillows. There were machines ranged around him, many of them beeping quietly. He had tubes in both arms but she was surprised to find he looked normal. He had colour in his face and seemed comfortable. There was no connection here with the blood-soaked body she had been with in the back of the screaming ambulance. His eyes were closed. Her heart fluttered at the sight of him, she willed his lids to rise. *Look at me Samuel, see me. I'm here, please look at me.*

By now the nurse had risen and crossed the room.

"Sorry love, you can't come in here. There's nothing you need to do. Just go back into the department, carry on with your other jobs."

She had to connect with him.

"Aw look, the poor thing, is he very sick?"

Maybe it would be enough, maybe if he heard her voice it would penetrate. His eyelids flickered. She took the chance.

"Hello love, I'm sorry you're not well."

As she spoke the nurse and policeman acted in unison, the nurse pushed at the door and the copper grabbed Sylvie's arm.

"I warned you, you're not to speak to him, come on. Move yourself."

"Alright mate, alright. I was just being nice."

His eyes opened, the noise and fuss had found its way through the mist surrounding him and he looked directly at her, she held her breath. Her eyes were stretched wide, she smiled and her hand rose of its own accord. He moved his head slightly, peered blearily at her and then his gaze swung to the nurse. The tube had been removed from his throat and he was parched.

"Could I have some water?"

The whispered words caught the nurse's attention and she stepped back towards her patient.

"It's alright, Samuel. I'll get your drink."

The policeman dragged at Sylvie, she had to try again, to find a way to attract his attention.

"Hey, take your hands off me. I'll sue you for assault."

Samuel turned his head, he looked into her eyes. His gaze swung away back to the nurse who offered him a tumbler with a straw poking from the top. There had been nothing, no sign of recognition, no flash of remembrance, absolutely nothing; he had looked through her. Her shoulders slumped as the tears leaped to her eyes, she had to cover the distress, had to get away. She was choking on emotion.

"Let go you sod, let go."

She ran from the room and through the unit, as she reached the main doors they swung open and she came

188

face to face with Constable Forbes flanked by the male detective who had questioned her in the waiting room.

"Sylvie." As she blurted the name Stella Forbes grabbed at the other girl. "What the hell."

Sylvie twisted and stamped on the other woman's foot and then she was off again, haring down these hospital corridors, running for her life as the alarms screeched around her.

Chapter 52

The flimsy shoe covers pinged from her feet and were left in a sad bundle with the hat she dragged from her head as she ran. She tore at the billowing coverall and threw it aside as she shot through the main doors. There were people after her – feet thudded on the tarmac of the roadway. She jigged and turned nipping between taxis and parked cars. An emergency vehicle screeched to a halt as she flew in front of it, she flung out her arms in reaction and it missed her by inches. Breath burned in her throat as she picked up speed. An old lady hobbling before her, leaning heavily on a metal walking frame, turned at the sound of running feet.

"Oh my word, whatever is it, what's wrong?"

She held out a hand as Sylvie flew past, "Hey, what have you done, why are you running away?"

They collided, only lightly but it was enough. The old woman tipped and stumbled.

"Oh, oh no." She tumbled to the pavement and the metal frame crashed into the road under the wheels of a passing car. The screech of tyres and the screams of the old woman lying on the ground beat into Sylvie's ears. She couldn't stop, mustn't stop; she ran on, away from the mayhem, her heart pounding and her gasping breath loud in her ears.

The chasing security guards had no choice but to stop, they had to help the old woman who had skinned her knees and the walking frame was tangled in the wheels of the car. The resultant back-up of traffic blocked the hospital entrance and an ambulance, lights flashing and siren blaring, mounted the pavement to try and find a way through the confusion.

Sylvie ran on and on, she didn't remember the way from last time but again her instinct took her out from the city centre. When she felt sure she had truly left all the pursuers behind she stopped and flopped to the ground beside a brick wall. She drew up her legs and lowered her head to her knees. Every bit of her body was shaking, her throat burned and her head pounded. She sat for many minutes simply waiting for her heart to resume a steady rhythm and for her brain to still and take stock of what had happened.

There was a tiny café on the corner of the road and she took herself inside to hide from the crowds and the day and the pure confusion of it all. She bought a bottle of water and asked for a cup of coffee. The table in the corner gave her a view of the window and the street outside but she felt hidden in the angle of the walls.

For a while she simply sat there trying to straighten out the events in her mind. Although going back there had been foolhardy, there was no denying she had needed to do it. Now she had seen him; he had looked better than expected, opened his eyes and was so very obviously improving. That was good, wasn't it? There was the other thing though, what could she take from that? He had looked straight at her, there was no doubt he had seen her but there had been nothing. Not in his eyes, not on his face, no sign at all that he knew her. In his condition and the flurry of those moments surely his reaction was unguarded and honest. So, did he truly not know her, or did he know her only too well?

Chapter 53

"Leave it, Forbes, there's plenty of bodies to catch her. Stay with me."

With the sharp instruction Detective Bailey swung back into the newly quieted room and dragged a chair to the bed where Samuel was struggling to keep his eyes open. He had been disturbed by the turmoil in his protected world and now turned to peer at this new visitor.

"Samuel. I'm Detective Bailey, this is Constable Forbes, we've been with you from the start of all this. I'm glad you're feeling a bit better, it must be great to have the tube out. The doctors have told us you can talk to us for a little while. If you find it all too much and want to stop at any time let me know and we can leave things for another day."

Samuel nodded and raised a hand.

"Marie, do you know where she is?"

The question was little more than a whisper and the desperation obvious in the sick man's eyes pulled at the detective's sympathy. He shook his head.

"There are a lot of things we are in a puzzle about, Samuel. I think if I tell you what we know as fact it might be a good place to start and then you can ask me whatever you want and I'll answer you where I can," Bailey said.

"You have to be aware though before we start, there has been a crime, we have a shooting, not only you but another man. We think we know who did it but we don't know why. At this moment in time you are not in any trouble but simply helping us with our investigation. Are you clear about that, Samuel? Don't try to talk just nod if you understand me," he continued.

He nodded.

"Do you remember being in the hotel?"

The question was answered with a weak shake of Samuel's head. He pointed at the plastic tumbler and Stella lifted it and helped him to drink.

"Okay, well we were called to The Seven Stars Hotel by someone reporting a disturbance. To save time I'll give you a quick rundown of what we found. We entered your room and you were lying in a pool of blood beside the bed, there was a girl with you, and there was the other man. I have to tell you he had also been shot and didn't survive."

"Marie, what about the baby? Are they okay?"

Now he was showing signs of being distraught, his breathing had grown rapid and laboured. One of the machines showed a red light where before there had been a green glow. The nurse hurried across the room.

"I'm not sure he's up to it. I think I should get the doctor."

Samuel reached out and grabbed at Stella's arm, "Tell me about Marie, is she okay? God why won't anyone tell me? Are they okay?"

The doctor pushed in beside the bed and nodded to the nurse who introduced a syringe full of medication into the infusion tube. Samuel calmed quickly and as his lids closed he made a final effort.

"Marie, will you fetch Marie?"

The police stood up, "Thanks for that, doc." The comment was sour and Bailey shook his head in frustration.

"I can't have him upset, I warned you when I agreed you could talk to him. You'll have to wait until he's stronger and that's all there is to it."

"Yeah, yes I know you're right it's just that we can't move along here. There were no documents, nothing to tell us who he is except the story from the girl and it's so frustrating. Nurse, do you know who this Marie is?"

"He's asked for her a few times and he keeps talking about a baby but according to the book there's been no-one visiting him and certainly no baby."

"Great, so we're even more confused than before. Anyway, let's address the other issue. Sylvie, how the hell did she get in here and what did she say to him?"

"I know nothing about her, I didn't recognise her, I've only been in the department two days and I thought she was the cleaner until she went ballistic when she saw you. Sorry can't help you."

"I don't expect she'll risk coming back but if she does, or anyone else for that matter, you need to let us know. Come on, Forbes, I'm feeling disgruntled I'm gonna tear a strip off the bloody plod who was sitting outside the door. I'm having his scalp."

"Hey, guv, he made a mistake, is all."

"Yeah well, I need a victim today and he's it."

Detective Bailey stormed from the room and could be heard a few minutes later, his voice a threatening growl as he harangued the hapless bobby who had allowed Sylvie access to the room.

As he drifted into the drug-induced peace, a great tear tracked down Samuel's cheek.

That had been so hard, unbelievably hard. He just wanted to drift away, he let go the strings of reality and as he fell into the peace, Marie came to him smiling.

Chapter 54

Sylvie left the little café with no idea where she was or what direction to take. This place was unfamiliar, busy and confusing and with the recent panic still raw, her brain refused to cling onto rational thoughts long enough to make decisions.

The image of Samuel as he looked at her in the room — looked through her really, as though she was a stranger — kept blocking out everything else. Every time she pictured his drowsy eyes filled with nothing but confusion she choked on the lump in her throat.

Was his brain damaged? How would she have been able to tell? She hadn't even had a moment before all hell had broken loose. Was he simply drugged, did he know her and want to protect her, or did he know her and want to protect himself with distance and ignorance? The thoughts pushed and jostled against each other as her legs carried her nervously through the hustle of the shopping streets.

Then, like a glimpse of a harbour from a storm-tossed sea she saw the figure, tall and skinny, striding out confidently before her, legs scissoring and long hair dancing from side to side.

"Lennie, Lennie wait."

The other woman spun and goggled at her in disbelief.

"Christ, Sylvie, how the hell did you get here? Bloody hell, talk about timing."

With this she grabbed hold of Sylvie by the arm and hustled her into a covered indoor market. Dragging her roughly along she ran down the narrow aisles, twisting this way and that, past vegetable stalls and butchery stands. She ran behind a counter piled high with carrots, cabbages and heaps of misshapen potatoes.

"Hiya, Stevo, back way open?"

The old man barely glanced up but he grinned and waved a hand towards the rear of the stall. Through the rough wooden door, they emerged into a walled yard filled with boxes, bins and cartons. Heaps of stinking and decaying vegetables filled the air with the stench of rot, Sylvie gagged on it as Lennie pulled her towards a narrow gateway, through and out into an alleyway.

For a moment now, in the dimness of this passage, Lennie turned and grabbed Sylvie by the arms her fingers digging into flesh still fragile with the abuse of just days ago. She spun her around until they were face to face.

"Bloody hell, how come you're here? I thought you were in the hossy with Aunty Marj. What happened?"

"I got into the room, Samuel was there, he was sitting up, well sort of and he looked okay really but then the police came and it all went pear-shaped and so I ran."

"Oh, oh well at least you saw him, so that's good yeah?"

"No, no he looked straight through me, he didn't even seem to recognise me at all, it was as if he'd never seen me before. It was horrible. Then I ran and this old woman fell over and there was chaos and I just kept on running. But what are you doing here, anyway? I can't believe I met you."

"Oh shit, I went to the pub. I couldn't rest wondering about you and so I went out. I was having a drink with a mate and then I saw 'em."

"Who, the police?"

"No, the police aren't after me, are they? Mo and Si, in their bloody great black car. They were just going round the corner I wouldn't have seen 'em except my mate was waving to his brother, anyway the point was they saw me and I freaked. I don't know what it was, just the look they gave me, so I came out to get away. I'm a bit scared about going back to the flat. I really am panicked, honest. I was going to hide at Marjie's."

"Oh no, what are we going to do now?"

"I don't know, I honestly don't. I had this idea. I was going to talk to you about it. I've had enough, I was wondering."

Here the girl paused, fighting to find the right words.

"I'm tired of it to be honest, Sylvie –all this. The fear and running and after what they did to you, the bastards. I'm sick to death of it. I think I want to put a stop to it."

"How, I mean what can you do, how can you stop it? I don't understand."

"The bizzies, I think we should go to the bizzies."

As Sylvie began to argue Lennie bent forwards and looked deep into her eyes.

"Think about it, love, just really think about it. You shot that bloke because he was going to rape you probably and he had shot your fella and you believed he would shoot you. Am I right?"

"Well, yes. Basically yes. But it was all the other stuff, the stuff Samuel was mixed up in and…" Now came the spectre of Phil, the violent scene in the little shack, the blood and horror. "Well there's other stuff as well." She paused.

When it came right down to it, she hadn't actually done anything. Yes, she had been there when Phil was killed – there was no denying it, but he had been beating her and

Samuel had protected her. As she thought of him then, saving her and taking all the responsibility, hot tears flowed from her over-cried eyes.

"Let me think, can you let me think about it all?"

"Of course! Look we can get to Aunty Marjie's house down here. Let's go there, have a brew and take some time. We need to let Marj know you're okay anyway and we should be alright there. We need to move though, love, if we're gonna do this thing we need to do it now. Mo and Si are evil buggers and if they're up here again so soon, you can bet they're up to no good. Come on."

They scurried together down the alleyway and then, with Lennie in the lead, they made their way to a little terraced house in a narrow street with cars lining both sides and children playing on the pavement.

Chapter 55

"Hello again, Samuel. How are you?"

"A bit better, I sat in the chair for a while. My head...
well I don't know."

Samuel's big hands covered his face. They had told him
tearfulness was all part of his illness and not to worry but it
was still embarrassing for him to cry in front of the
detective. Peter Bailey sat quietly with his eyes lowered,
giving the other man time to collect himself.

"Well, let's hope we can clear up some of the puzzles
for you. We know who you are now. You'd already been
told I think."

Samuel nodded. "Yes, bits have come back as well. I
still don't know though about Marie and the baby. I've
asked the nurses and the doctors about them and all they
did was to tell me to wait for you. They said you have all
the information. I don't understand it, where is she? Do
you know? Have you found her?" Emotion overwhelmed
him, his voice cracked and for a moment the power of
speech deserted him.

He coughed and tried again, "I thought I'd seen her,
just a few days ago, but they said it wasn't possible and it
was all part of the coma." Now it was too much and he

cried, openly and unashamed. "I'm sorry, I just need her. We should be together; I don't believe we had a break up, nothing like that. I just want her here with me."

Detective Bailey waited for the storm to pass, he had spoken to the medical people and understood there was no way to predict what would come back or how long it would take. There was nothing to do but wait and there was no point in trying to predict the outcome for Samuel.

The house in The Lakes was clear in Samuel's mind. He had already related many memories from his childhood. He had recalled his mum and dad, could talk about their death, and times when he had lived in the house with Marie. They had prepared a nursery. He could describe in fine detail the wallpaper, the cot and baby furniture just as if he'd been there a short while ago. He could remember much of his time in the army and serving overseas. When they asked him about the time after the army there was a gap, he couldn't explain how and why he left and then it was as if a line had been drawn. His life was on one side, and then this pain and the hospital and confusion. In between there was a void, empty and puzzling and Marie had fallen into it.

Samuel raised his head and tried a quiver of a smile, "Sorry, I feel such a wuss."

The man sitting before him with a large plastic file on his knee simply shook his head. Samuel's eyes were drawn to the file, he knew the answers were in there and he also knew his life, such as it was in this unfinished state, was going to be changed when the plastic covers were opened.

"So, we have the papers from the army, your rank, service record and so on. All okay there, nothing to worry about, impressive really. I'll leave a copy with you so you can have a read."

Now it was coming, the other man fidgeted on the hard seat, he had made a decision and looked Samuel in the face, a direct gaze. It was kind and it was sympathetic and Samuel readied himself.

"I'm sorry, we have found out about Marie. It's in here." He lifted the plastic folder. "It was the reason you left the army. She was killed, I'm really sorry. She was killed in a car accident and afterwards they let you resign on compassionate grounds."

He waited then for just a moment before reaching across to touch Samuel on the hand.

"I am really sorry. It's awful for you that you had forgotten; I can't imagine how this must feel. We have a police report about it and the army records. I have read them all and you should ask me anything you want. Or, if you'd rather I can just leave it with you."

Samuel gulped, shook his head as if he was trying to clear it and then he spoke quietly.

"The baby?"

"No, sorry there was no baby. Marie was pregnant when she was killed but there was no baby, well not born if you understand."

"Can you leave me? Can I be on my own?"

"Yes, of course. Look I'll come back later. I'm really sorry but there is still a lot we have to clear up. There is Sylvie, apart from anything else," Bailey said.

"Who?"

"Sylvie."

Again the shake of his head.

"I don't know anyone called Sylvie. Who is she?"

"The girl who was with you in the hotel, the one who broke in the other day, dressed as a cleaner. Samuel, she was the one who shot the other bloke. We don't know but it seems as though maybe she saved your life."

"No, no sorry. I don't know anyone called Sylvie. Never did and I can't remember anything about the day I was shot. I don't even know what I was doing in the hotel, I don't know why I am here in Liverpool. I just don't know."

With this desperate statement he lowered his head into his hands and the grief overwhelmed him.

After a few moments Detective Bailey pushed back the chair and left the room. Contrary to what he had just said he didn't leave the folder, the contents made difficult reading, he didn't believe Samuel was strong enough. There were the descriptions of the accident, the accounts of Samuel's breakdown and then just a statement that he was discharged on compassionate grounds. The army paid his pension but the account had never been used. There was the house in The Lake District and the people who had been interviewed there said Samuel had disappeared after the funeral and nobody had seen him since. A cleaner was paid regularly by electronic means but she hadn't communicated directly with Samuel for a long time.

The house had been broken into a short while ago but there had been no damage, so the cleaner had simply cleaned up, throwing out the few things left there and carried on. She hadn't even bothered to report it as she had no faith in the police investigating such a small crime.

There was so very much unexplained and of course one of the major items was the great holdall full of money. The cash had been unmarked and though they had tried, they hadn't found any clues about the source. This being the case the money belonged to Samuel. Yes, there had been traces of cocaine but they were so minimal as to be meaningless. The landlady of the hotel had told them he paid in cash, from a large bag and there it was. Perhaps there was a drug connection but what, where, when and who, was proving impossible to discover.

Samuel was a reasonably wealthy man, with a house in one of the most beautiful parts of the world. His bank account was very healthy due to the regular payments and in truth he would probably never have to work again. Knowing this, Detective Bailey still wouldn't change places with this grieving, lonely, damaged individual even if he had to work until the day he dropped dead.

Chapter 56

"He didn't even know who I was. Either he really didn't recognise me or he didn't want me there, I don't know which but I couldn't ever bear to see such a look on his face again. He looked straight through me. It's over, for me and him. I'm sure it's over.

"So, what is it, what's your idea?"

Sylvie was sitting on the couch, exhausted mentally and physically. Her heart was leaden, every time she thought of Samuel and the blank and unknowing expression in his eyes she wanted to curl into a ball and wail and thrash and rail at the unfairness of life. After all the years of mixing with dead beats and dangerous criminals, she had found him. When he told her he was on the run she had pushed the knowledge aside. Deep in her soul she believed he was a good man and the story of loss and tragedy he told her reinforced that belief.

She gave herself to him totally, the sex had been good and within it she had chosen to believe there was genuine feeling and caring, maybe even love. If it was the case surely, no matter how ill he was and how afraid, he would have known her, something would have been carried over from then to now.

It seemed she had been wrong and now she was alone. This was not a new situation. In the other life, before Samuel, she had been on her own but in her own place, she had a life there. It hadn't been much of a life but it was hers, now there was nothing. No home, the clothes she stood up in and the tiny bit of money in her bank account and that was it. Nothing to hold, nothing to hope for and nothing to lose.

So, she sat back against the slightly greasy cover of Lennie's auntie's sofa and opened herself up to what the other girl had to say.

"I've been running from Si and Mo for a long time. Since before Brian died, yeah long before. They're thugs and lowlifes but they have money and power and I think they are part of something big, really big. I hate the bizzies, never had anything to do with 'em that came out well, but I've been thinking. This is never going to go away, now I'm mixed up with you I feel I've been sucked further in," Lennie said.

Sylvie gasped at this and leaned forward. Lennie shook her head and wrapped an arm around her shoulders.

"Don't worry I don't blame you, I really don't. With you all I feel is guilt, really deep guilt. When I saw what they'd done to you, in the warehouse, well I could have died. I can't let this go on any longer. What will they have me doing next, eh? How far will they make me go? No. It stops here. It has to because I think if I don't do something, I'll end up dead," she continued.

"I thought we could go to the cops, you and me. We can make up a story, we'll tell them you were raped, tell them you had to shoot that bloke because he was going to kill you and your Samuel. Maybe they'll do a witness protection thing. I know where they go when they're here, Si and Mo and some others. I know where they keep their stuff. Don't ask me how because I won't tell you but I know and I know other stuff as well – stuff the filth might really like to know. Honest, there are bodies I know about, there are girls as well, girls locked up and abused. I know where they are. I wouldn't have ever gone on my own it's too scary, but I will if you come with me. What do you think?"

The tears wouldn't be dammed any longer and they flooded down Sylvie's cheeks. She lowered her head into her hands and sobbed as life disintegrated around her. All the new hope, the fresh happiness and the blossoming love washed away in this grimy house in a strange town in the bony arms of a stranger and she let it go, what choice did she have? She just let it go.

"What will I do afterwards though, where will I go. I'm so scared, I try to see what will happen and there's nothing. I can't even imagine tomorrow. It's like I'm falling, deeper and deeper into some sort of great hole and it's bottomless and endless. I don't want to end on the streets; I don't want to go on the game and just don't understand how this has all happened," Sylvie said.

Even now, in the deepest despair she couldn't tell Lennie about Phil. She had buried it so deep that if she spoke his name, related the events of that dark and ghastly night, then all the hounds of hell would be loosed and the chaos it caused would be unstoppable. Could she carry this secret with her forever, locked in her soul, a dark and dreadful pulse to be borne until her last moments and then what, to carry it still into whatever there was beyond this reality? Would it not drive her insane, never sharing, holding it close and keeping it part of her forever? Was it possible to have any sort of life, happiness and hope with such baggage? She would never know unless she tried and right now there was no other road to take and so she gulped back the fear, looked into Lennie's eyes and nodded.

They didn't hug or smile, this was no time for a high five, they were two frightened desperate women hanging on and trying to keep going. And so they sat quietly in the little house and lost themselves in their own thoughts and tried to summon the courage to move on.

"What about Samuel though, what will happen to him do you think?"

"I don't know love, I really don't. If he can't remember you, maybe he can't remember anything at all about the past and then what will they do? If he can't remember and they can't prove anything well it could be all right. I know you don't want to hear it just now but leaving him might be the biggest favour you could do him. Maybe it's for the best in the end and it's the way it has to be. He hasn't been arrested has he? They seem to be looking after him well. Maybe he'll be okay and it's better like this, for him and for you. D'ya think?"

Sylvie nodded slowly, could this be what was meant to happen? Though it had wrapped her in barbs of guilt until the day she died, it had freed Samuel and right now perhaps that was enough. For him to be free to live in his lovely house in The Lake District and to find peace in the turmoil of his life would make some sort of sense after all.

Chapter 57

The quiet was overwhelming, street sounds and the ticking clock underlined their inability to make more conversation. With no further excuse to stay, Lennie stood and picked up her bag and jacket, she scribbled a note for her aunty and turned to her friend.

"Come on, love. We should go and if we're gonna do this thing I think we should do it now. They're out there, I've seen 'em today and I'm scared."

Sylvie nodded and together they left the little house, casting glances back and forth. Their nervousness grew sharply the longer they were in the open. The route twisted and turned down the back alleys and narrow streets as they scuttled back to the flat.

"We need a story. It has to be simple and we both need to be able to stick to it no matter what. I know there are things you haven't told me and it's okay, I have enough stuff of my own to cart about, I don't need any more garbage..."

Lennie's lips lifted in a smile which didn't reach her eyes. She plonked two mugs of coffee down on the carpet and flung herself against the bean bag. A great sigh lifted her shoulders and then she stiffened. "Okay, let's get on with it."

Sylvie sipped at her coffee before asking, "All this stuff you say you know, how sure are you about it all? I mean if we go to the police and then they don't find what you say, it'll all fall apart."

"Oh, believe me I know." Lennie visibly paled and she hugged herself, this reaction stilled any more questions from Sylvie. She didn't want to know, the horrors she carried were enough for her, she had no room for more.

"So, what do you think, do we ring them? Go to the police station? Once we do, they will have me, won't they? There'll be no way back." Sylvie grasped the other woman's hand, "I'm scared, I am really scared."

"I know, love, I know but I can't think what else to do. I'm not going to force you, course I'm not, but I think I have to do it, for me. If you want to run, leave me to it then I wouldn't blame you, I would never blame you."

"I have nowhere to go, I have no-one to be with, except you and this has got to finish..."

"Christ what was that noise?" The crash of the front door brought them both to their feet.

The interior door slammed against the wall and bounced back to hit the fist of the man glowering in the doorway. Behind him the dark shadow of a second male reinforced the threat and drew a shriek of fear from Sylvie. Lennie for her part simply muttered under her breath. "Oh God."

The two women had stepped instinctively toward each other, their hands joined. Terrified eyes watched as the two thugs stepped over the threshold and pushed the door closed behind them.

"Ladies." Si bent from the waist, a mocking parody of chivalry.

Lennie could feel Sylvie's fingers shuddering with fear and heard her rapid panting. Her stomach had clenched and bile filled her throat, this was it. She had known really that a face off was inevitable but she had turned away from the belief and carried on in false hope.

"How are you, Lennie? And you, slut, getting better are you? Ready for some more fun perhaps?" He turned. "What do you reckon, Mo, d'ya think you'd like a bit more party." He jabbed a finger towards where Sylvie was fighting to keep it together, her instincts told her to scream and run but her eyes showed her there was nowhere to go. She clung to Lennie's damp hand and waited.

"Yeah, maybe. Mind she wasn't very good, not last time, a bit dull if I remember. Lennie now, well we can always rely on Lennie, what'ya say girl, ready for a bit a jiggy?" He moved into the room, pushing past his friend and stepping to where the two women were pressed now against the wall.

Si glanced around, "How do you live here, really how? It's shit. Did you know that, Lennie? You live in shit. But then how would you know, eh? It's all you've ever lived in, isn't it? Pigs in shit, you and your worthless brother, your junkie waste of skin, Brian. Oh, oh no, he isn't living in shit anymore is he, Lennie?"

When it came none of them were ready, it was a sudden and violent explosion. Sylvie had been aware of Lennie's fingers clenching and unclenching and she felt the body beside her tense and tighten but when the other girl moved the force of it knocked her to her knees on the grubby carpet.

She looked up in bewilderment as the streak of violence which had once been Lennie screamed across the room and connected with Si. Fists, nails and teeth raked, bit, punched and slapped. Si, caught unprepared as he was, could do no more than raise his hands to try and protect his eyes. Lennie didn't let it stop her, she had taken all she could take and now the fury and fear drove her on.

Even as the blood began to trickle from the deep gouges on his cheeks she grabbed at his ears and, screaming now with the passion of it, she pulled at them and stretched in towards him to bite and tear with her teeth.

He screamed, "Mo, for God's sake, Mo, get her off me." As the other man made his move Sylvie came to her senses, these were the men who had punished her so badly and now there was a chance for revenge. Grabbing the lamp from the little side table she smashed the bulb against the wall and approached the roiling mass of skin, flesh and fury at the other side of the room. She jabbed and poked with the sharp edges of glass catching both Mo and Si in turn, driving them back away from the sobbing, gulping Lennie who followed the retreating thugs, still kicking and thumping. Blind with fury, totally beyond any sort of control she was an unstoppable force.

As Si tried to grab her hands, she brought her knee up to his groin with all the force her scrawny body could manage. Behind the action was years of pain and grief and when it found its mark, Si screamed as his world dissolved into red pain and he fell to his knees gasping and groaning.

Mo was struggling now with Sylvie, trying to wrench the lamp from her hands but she whirled and spun jabbing at him with the glass-sharp end and he leapt back again and again unable to penetrate the wall of hate. Lennie's legs were working now, she still had on her boots and she kicked and stamped on the groaning Si, his back, his head, his belly over and over. She was sobbing and grunting like some demented creature and long after he lay still, she continued to beat at the ruined unconscious thing he had become.

Sylvie for her part was weakening against the strength of Mo, he was too much for her. She was a small thing and he was sturdy and fit. It was a match doomed to failure from the very moment it started. Once the light bulb had disintegrated, he simply dragged the lamp from the girl's hands and threw it aside. With a glance at his fallen comrade and with a chilling calm he spun to face where Sylvie backed away from him retreating into the corner by the window. He followed her, two steps brought him to where she was pressed against the dowdy walls and as he stretched his great hands towards her, she understood that she was lost.

With a piercing screech Lennie launched herself across the room and flung herself back into the fray. Had she come from behind it would have been a lost cause but coming sideways she caught Mo mid step, off-balance and he tipped towards the bed. As his legs connected with the metal frame, she pressed home her advantage, leaping onto his body, wrapping her arms around his shoulders and taking him down with the weight and force of her forward motion. He fell partly onto the bed and then squirming to drag himself from under the screaming furious woman he slid further to slouch against the frame. Sylvie re-joined the fight. She picked up the table, scattering the bottles and mirror across the floor and with a wild yell she brought the heavy wood down onto Mo's head. Still it wasn't enough to defeat him and he grabbed at the broken furniture flinging it aside even as he struggled to regain his feet.

Lennie tore aside the curtain separating the kitchen from the living room. She dragged open a narrow drawer and snatched up the big carving knife. Without a beat of hesitation, she flew across the small space the blade brandished before her and with no thought as to where it would pierce, she jabbed and stabbed at what had been but short moments before an arrogant and powerful male. Now, reduced to a bloody mess he fell back against the bed, red flooded from his belly which he clutched with slick and desperate hands. He raised his eyes to hers, the look in them was fear, disbelief and hatred and then they clouded and a great and sudden silence engulfed the shabby flat.

Chapter 58

By the time the police arrived Si was groaning and rolling on the bloodstained carpet. Emergency workers were trying to help him but he fought and struggled with them. He was semi-conscious and bleeding from his ears and nose. His face was a mass of bruises, his lips were split, they thought some ribs were broken. The paramedics were trying to calm him and prevent further harm. Lennie watched with dead eyes wondering just what damage she had been able to inflict, hoping it was extensive and permanent.

The bloke from the lower flat was hovering near the door. The look on his face said he would rather be anywhere but there. He had thundered up the stairs and come upon the scene of devastation without really thinking. Though he was completely out of his depth, he was glad he had 'done something' for his friend without being required to risk actual physical harm. He had dialled 999 and started the whole reaction but now he wanted to go. He had wrapped Sylvie and Lennie in the duvet and blanket from the bed. The dead body had appalled and terrified him and he had simply let it be and the mess that was Si had overwhelmed him. He had tried to put a pillow under the man's head but Lennie's scream had stopped him.

"Don't! Don't even touch him, the bastard. Leave him be, Davey, let him die."

The two women were side by side on the edge of the bed. Both were shaking with shock and the effects of the adrenaline rush. Their hands were clasped on top of the mattress and now and again Sylvie gave a quiet sob.

Sylvie hoped the police presence might include the detective she already knew. In her befuddled mind it seemed maybe it would help. They had not had a chance to formulate a plan and she had no idea what Lennie was going to say. Now, if the detective and constable arrived then she would simply hand over to them. *"Here I am, take me and do what you will. I am finished and can't fight anymore."*

Lennie wasn't ready to give in so easily and immediately the senior police officer, a stranger, approached them and introduced himself, she launched into a tirade.

"Get them buggers out of my place, shift em. Christ you're not even safe in your own home any more. What are you lot doing letting scum like that roam the streets? You just think yourself lucky you haven't got more bodies to deal with, mate. It's a miracle we aren't raped and dead." She seemed to crumble then, her shoulders heaved as she gulped and sniffed. Sylvie moved across the bed and cradled her, as they leaned in together Lennie whispered urgently, "Keep your mouth shut, don't say anything."

She nodded imperceptibly.

"Are either of you hurt? Do you need a doctor or to go to the hospital? I can call another ambulance."

"No, we want to stay here, we want to be together and we want you to get that filth away from us." If this was an act then Lennie was giving a stunning performance, but beneath it all Sylvie knew there was real fear and true hate.

"I'm sorry, Lennie, it is Lennie isn't it?"

The girl nodded.

"I can't move them that quickly. I think it's best if you and your friend come with us."

"Where, where do you want us to go? I'm not going to no bloody lock up, you can forget that. No way mate."

"No, no. Just come with us we'll take you to the station, we have a room there where you can be quiet. We can get you some tea, a doctor to check you over if you need it. It's just not possible for you to stay here. We have to ask you some questions, you must know that and you need to get out of this place. Will you come?"

"You're not arresting us or nothing?"

"No, we're not. We just need to be able to do our work here and we need to get you away from this mess. Will you come?"

The girls glanced at each other, Sylvie could see Lennie was trying to convey urgent messages, so she simply clamped her mouth shut and her lead the way.

"Okay, but we want to stay together, we need each other."

"We will need to take statements; you can't do it together. Come on, Lennie, you know how this works don't you?" The comment told them, though he was trying to be kind, the policeman wasn't totally taken in by the act.

Lennie nodded and on shaking legs they allowed themselves to be led to the waiting car.

Chapter 59

With dull cream walls and a tiny window, the room was small and institutional. Sylvie was sitting on a plastic chair. The police had been kind, had offered them tea and access to a doctor. They had been in another room, carpeted and furnished with soft chairs and with pictures on the walls. Now she was alone. Lennie was probably in a similar little box elsewhere in the station. The detective had been gentle but firm, they needed statements and to do it the girls had to be separate. They hadn't left them alone together since the flat.

The door opened and Detective Bailey walked in flanked by a constable in uniform.

"Hello again, Sylvie." He threw a plastic file onto the table and dragged up a chair. "Are you okay?"

She nodded.

"Well, you have been leading us a bit of a dance, haven't you?" He tipped his head to one side, he wasn't threatening but she couldn't trust him, couldn't trust herself. She tried to swallow but her throat was parched.

"Can I have a drink, some water?"

"Of course. Constable, would you?"

"Are you better now?"

"Thanks, yes."

"Okay. Where do we start? Well, why don't you tell me why you ran? I don't understand at all. You were so concerned, in the hospital, distraught really and then you just left him, Samuel. We can't make any sense of it."

"Is he okay, Samuel?"

"He's not doing badly at all. He's out of the woods anyway."

"Has he mentioned me?"

"No, he hasn't and this is where it is all so very confusing. You told us you were an item. The landlady at the hotel said you were like 'Love's young dream', her words! But he doesn't remember you and you left him in intensive care fighting to live. Doesn't really gel now does it?"

Sylvie shook her head. She had to manage this, had to fashion a history to fit with what had happened. She coughed.

"I know, I know. I think maybe I was a bit, well you know, over enthusiastic. I was so worried about him and I thought if I told you we had only just got together you wouldn't let me stay."

"Okay. So why not tell me all about it and then we can maybe move on?"

"Yes, yes I will. He gave me a lift, I told you I met him in a bar and it's true. I wanted to come here and he gave me a lift. It started then but..." Here she shrugged and gave a little grin. "Well you know, he was nice, really kind and we were in the car for a long time. We had to stay overnight in it. Well, do I need to spell it out?"

"No, probably not. How long were you together then?"

"A few days that's all. But he was so nice and then he brought me here, well he was bringing me. He's got a house, in the Lakes and we stayed there and then he said he'd bring me here, I wanted to visit Liverpool. Anyway, the car broke down, he had to leave it on the motorway, we hitched in a truck and then we found the hotel."

"The man you shot?"

"I don't know, I really don't." Her hands were clenched on the table top the knuckles white with tension. Her shoulders were hunched, she was a picture of misery.

"We went into town; it was nice and we had a good time. Then we went back to the room and that man was there. I didn't understand any of it. I don't know if Samuel knew him but anyway, oh God. It all got out of hand and he shot Samuel, he beat me up and I thought he was going to rape me. I shot him, I told you, didn't I? Already, I told you I shot him. Will I go to jail? Am I a murderer?"

"If you don't think Samuel knew the man, why do you think he was there, in the room?"

"I don't know, I honestly don't know."

The detective sighed. "These other men, the ones from today in Lennie's flat. Who are they?"

"You'll have to ask, Lennie. I don't know about them. Lennie's lovely she helped me but those men have been following her and I just got mixed up in it. Is Lennie okay?"

"She's fine. She's being very helpful. I think the things she knows are going to be very important. You though, you don't know anything about Si and Mo, where they came from or who they are?"

Oh yes, I know, I know they were animals, I know that no matter what, I'm glad we hurt them. I wish they were both dead – not just one of them. Oh yes, I know them."

She simply shook her head and shrugged.

"Okay, I think that'll do for the moment anyway. Are you okay, do you need anything?"

"I'm all right. What's going to happen to me though, am I going to jail?"

"Well, let's just say that if your mate Lennie has anything to do with it neither of you will be going anywhere near a jail."

He smiled at her and left her on her own in an agony of worry in the plain little place. She was cut off from the world, separated from her friend and, she knew now, totally divorced from any sort of life with Samuel. She sat back against the hard plastic. Maybe it didn't matter, she'd had so very little to lose.

Chapter 60

The wait was endless and frustrating and frightening. They brought her food and took her to the bathroom when she asked. They checked on her regularly but they told her nothing.

As the light through the little window faded to grey, she lay her head on her arms across the table and closed her eyes and tried to sleep. She drifted in and out of a doze, snippets of memory teasing at the edges of her mind. Samuel, tireless, driving through the night, the flight across the fell and the terror in the motorway services. The Lakes and Liverpool and horror. It was the horror that brought her head up from the table in a jerk, the feel of the chair under her and the stiffness in her back and legs. She glanced around, it was okay, and she was okay.

Before it was fully dark Bailey came back, with another policeman to stand at the door. "Right. I'm sorry you've been waiting so long, it's complicated and these things take time."

"What things?"

"That's what I'm here to talk to you about. We've been with Lennie, as you know. She's given us plenty to think about and we've come to an arrangement."

"Am I going to jail?"

He held up his hand.

"Wait, just listen. The stuff with Samuel still bothers me, but he says he doesn't know who you are, you say it was a casual thing between the two of you and there doesn't seem to be any way forward with it all. In light of everything else I have to tell you I think you can pretty much put that behind you." He opened the file and shuffled papers.

"Now then, Si and Mo, Lennie pretty much backed up what you said. You got mixed up in this by accident, but now you are mixed up in it, aren't you? These people are not nice, not nice at all and they won't be happy with what's gone on. I have to say that you're in trouble."

Sylvie drew in a sharp breath, this was it then, she was going to jail.

He continued, "You need to be made safe."

"Safe?"

"Yes, we can't just let you walk out of here and carry on. Lennie has to be looked after, she's been very brave, a bit late admittedly but," he shrugged, "We will take care of her, she's going into what we call witness protection and she's going to carry on helping us."

"Oh, but me. What about me? I can't help you; I don't know anything."

"Well, not as much as she does it's true but, you know some things. You were at the flat and that has put you in danger. It's possible they'll come after you, when they can't find Lennie, they'll assume that you know where she is. Anyway, to get to the point here, if you are willing, we can offer you the same deal as we've offered her. We can help you to get away. We can set you up somewhere and try to keep you safe."

"Where, where can I go?"

He grinned across the table at her now.

"Well your mate has come up with a couple of ideas, most of which were out of the question but we think we've found something we can work with. It's not easy this you know. You won't be able to contact your family or friends. You won't be able to go back to where you used to live. You have to go away, right away and forget your past, your history. Do you think you could do that?"

"I don't have any. No family, not really, and nobody I want to see. Could I go with Lennie though, if she wants me to, she's the only friend I've had for years. Do you think I could do that?"

"Well, I have to tell you that she was pretty insistent that you go together. She's a tough one your friend, but yes, I think we can sort this. Now we're taking you somewhere nicer than this, you'll be safe there and you can have a sleep and then, well we'll get things moving."

"Samuel?"

"It's over, that's over, he doesn't remember you anyway and you're best letting that go. It was only a bit of a fling anyway wasn't it, from what you said." His face gave nothing away but she wasn't fooled, he knew, he understood that there was something there and that was the thing that she had to let go, not friends, not family but whatever it had been with Samuel.

Chapter 61

Lennie swung around and dragged Sylvie into a great hug. The other girl grinned back, her eyes glittered as she peered around in disbelief at the glorious sunshine, the rows of palm trees and the unbelievably blue arch of sky.

"I can't believe it, I really can't. Are we really in Spain; honestly Spain?"

"I know, I know. Hey that guy there has my name on a board."

"No, he doesn..." here they dissolved into slightly hysterical giggles. Hanging on to each other they approached the taxi driver.

"Senorita Lynne. I am your driver, you can come with me, si?"

"Si, yes we can. Do you know where you're taking us?"

"Si, the village, the Bodega Seven Stars. You are the new owner I think."

"Yes, me and my friend, this is Stella. We are the new owners." The driver grinned at the little jump of excitement she gave. Okay, yet another English bar owner to thrive or fail in Spain but it didn't impact on him and she was so very excited only a hard man would fail to be amused. Her little friend, Stella, was quieter, more withdrawn. He gave a little shrug, maybe they would make it work, it wasn't his problem.

"I take you now to your flat yes, and then to the Bodega."

"Yes, yes thank you."

So it began, a new life, an escape for both of them, new names, new identities and, providing they could make it work, a new business to run. When Lennie had suggested to the police that she would like to have a bar in Spain it made sense. They both knew the ups and downs of bar work and Lennie was confident she could handle the rest of it. They had a new flat, passports, a little money, very little money in truth but they didn't care. It was up to them, for the first time either of them could remember they were in charge of their own destinies, so they strode out into the sunshine and followed the taxi driver to the airport car park. Their arms were linked, futures entwined and the past receding slowly, very slowly as the wounds healed and the hope grew.

* * *

They knew it wasn't quite over, as part of the deal they had sworn to give evidence at the trials. Lennie more than Sylvie was under an obligation that would run for many years. They would be disguised; they wouldn't even be in the court rooms, probably not even in England. It would be done by video links and as much as possible would be done to protect their new identities. They were determined to do it. They acknowledged that for a long time yet there was a small risk. The tentacles of the drug gang were long and intertwined with many businesses and authorities, but they'd had nothing to lose and they had judged it a small price to pay for this once-in-a-lifetime chance for a new beginning.

* * *

After he left the hospital and moved back home Samuel was driven by a great need. His recovering body worked against him and it was weeks before he could make the journey. Some of his neighbours offered to drive, but when he did it everything must be right. No car, no company, just himself. At last he felt strong enough and so he rose at dawn and packed a bag. The house was a home again now, it would never be what it had been but it was a haven and it was enough.

Down the path and out of the wooden gate, he turned to the rise of land beyond the little stone wall. There was a tug in his memory of a dark night, screaming tyres and danger, but he let it go, today was about renewal and moving forward. He lifted his face to the sun and breathed the thin air of the Lakeland springtime. His newly recovered muscles warmed with the activity and the long hike became a pleasure. He stopped often and absorbed the peace and the glory before walking on steadily.

Several hours later he turned into a gateway, past discreet signage and understated buildings. There was a place in the porch to leave his bag and stow his walking shoes. His stockinged feet made small sounds on the slate floor as he slipped into the little chapel to light two candles, one for each soul. After a brief rest on the pale wooden bench in the dappled quiet he resumed the journey. Out again into the sunshine and down a bark-strewn path into the edge of the woods. He was unfaltering; though it was a large area he knew just where it was, how it lined up against the distant hills and the bend in the river, this spot was burned into his memory and he knew he would always find it. She was here.

He laid his hand on the turf. She was with him now, he sensed it. The sun was warm against his back and before him lake, meadow and hamlet basked in the northern light.

His spirit had lifted with each step; it felt good to be here. Now he let the tears flow, there was no-one to see them and anyway he didn't care, after the horror that his life had been this honest emotion was cleansing.

There were no markings, it was a gentle slope of woodland, a tiny stream danced and sparkled at the edge of his vision. He loved this burial ground for its beauty and for the precious thing beneath the earth. She was sleeping here, cradling their unborn child forever.

"I'm so sorry, Marie, I'm so very sorry." He had loved her and had no doubt she had loved him. Surely love accepts and forgives and though things he had done had been dreadful and wicked, this was a second chance. The betrayal and the forfeit of the other burgeoning love had been a great sacrifice but he had grasped the opportunity and could only hope he had been right. He would have preferred that the price paid had been exacted from him alone but it wasn't to be.

He glanced around, it felt that he was alone but he knew that one day they would come. They would find him and he would have to deal with it and it may cost him his life, but so be it. He could have gone away again, another new start, anywhere, at the other side of the world if he had wanted, but he was tired of running. He'd wanted to come home and rest in the peace and so he had.

As the sun began to dip and the blackbird took to the treetops to sing to the evening, he uncurled and pushed to his feet. He touched his fingers to his lips and dropped a kiss upon the earth where his wife and child slept. Turning away he faced the evening glow, bowed his head and whispered to the breeze. "And you, Sylvie, I'm so very sorry, forgive me." With the gloaming song of the bird filling the air and the sky bleeding crimson into the distant lake, Samuel stepped away from the grave and took the first steps towards whatever was coming.

The End

If you enjoyed this book, please let others know by leaving a quick review on Amazon. Also, if you spot anything untoward in the paperback, get in touch. We strive for the best quality and appreciate reader feedback.

editor@thebookfolks.com

www.thebookfolks.com

Made in the USA
Monee, IL
30 August 2019